I0630404

Affections in the Star-Flagged Land

Dani Santos Lang

ISBN 979-8-9864448-1-9

This book is dedicated to my best American friend. James, my love, my husband, my other half.

S trange having no place, but finding yourself, even so, within yourself. And from the connections made—some broken, some supported by concrete and, at the same time, intangible matter—only what is essential remains. It is the nature of living—neither good nor bad; it just is. And life itself doesn't even touch eternity; just like the seasons, the love, the disaffections, all totalities, it, one day, also ends.

A little bit of winter

I n my early twenties, I took advantage of my few privileges and embarked on a new life. I wasn't seeking professional success, nor did I want to "find myself." I wasn't chasing anything, I just wanted to turn a page of my story. I had nothing against my country. On the contrary, I loved the fact that I was born there; I loved my people, my language, and my traditions. Brazil, the land of infinite beauty, welcoming people and hidden truths—the best and the worst place on earth. But I decided to leave it to explore what was on the other side of things. And I started by seeing how the "American dream" nation would treat me.

I arrived in New York City at Christmas time. The snow, so beautiful in the movies, wasn't as glamorous in person. Pushed from the streets to the side of the road to allow the safe circulation of vehicles, it mixed with the dirt of the asphalt, and its whiteness was tarnished. I soon realized that my tropical-country winter clothes wouldn't be enough. The cold of minus I-don't-know-how-many degrees Celsius hurt my lips and hands. The dry weather gave me static shocks every time I touched the gate of the building I lived in. But it wasn't all bad. The lights, the Christmas shows, the ice-skating rinks brought certain comfort to the heart.

My apartment was tiny and far from the iconic places in the city, but the subway took me everywhere—this, of course, after I learned to decipher it and to pretend that the filth and the rats didn't bother me. My master's classes would start in the spring, and in the meantime, I'd wait tables, babysit, and even scrub toilets now and then to make some money.

During my entire first month there, I felt like I was in a movie, but as an observer. And my identity sometimes raised questions within me; I kept trying to remember "who I was." What language could define me best? The taste for strong coffee got mixed with the desire for pancakes with syrup in the morning, and the days passed like a mist in an almost dreamlike atmosphere.

My only company was my roommate, and I managed to have trivial conversations with her, which soon faded into thin air. Our minds worked in different ways, and despite being friendly and smiling at each other, we didn't really have a connection. I felt alone, but that didn't really bother me much. I had always been alone, after all.

I spent my first many days, when I wasn't working, visiting the city, so loved and so hated at the same time, like any big metropolis. As for me, I still didn't quite know how I felt about it—there's no choice of how to feel, actually, so full of diversity was that place. New York revealed itself differently every day, in every corner. It could be a prude one moment and a whore the next. Artistic, with its bearded guys and tattooed girls, its musicals and museums. Superficial, with its strip bars, clubs, and imaginary acid trips. It stank of urine and Chanel No. 5. I had fun trying to decipher my new home. I went to all the must-see places for newcomers, of course, and it was surreal to be there, seeing in person what was on travel agency flyers. Of course, not everything impressed me. The Statue of Liberty, for example. In my mind, it was this majestic symbol of the American nation's power: imposing, almost divine. But on reaching the island (even before that, seeing it from afar from the boat), I felt as if I had lost a mental erection. Lady Liberty was small—in size and majesty. She didn't intimidate me—I even shot her a defiant look, and she just stared back at me with her dead eyes.

My favorite place was Central Park—a piece of nature amidst the concrete. I liked to sit there on the grass and fill myself with that energy. There were always children playing, sometimes with their dogs, and also couples holding hands, families having picnics. And there were the loners, of course. People with their books, their tai chi, their meditation, their headphones...

There, I felt the rebirth of an inspiration that had abandoned me many years before. It was just another Sunday, and the sun comforted me with its warmth—in the shade, the freezing cold still prevailed. I was trying to concentrate on a book, but something made me uneasy. I didn't quite know what. I put it aside and looked around without expectations. A strangely warm breeze caught my attention. It brought me a flower petal. Red, alive; it landed on my leg. I picked it up—it smelled like hope. Amid the dry, ugly trees, bruised by the winter, that single petal made me smile. It brought back a childhood memory. Around eight years old, at school, while the other kids were playing on the playground after lunch, I was sitting with a coloring book, very busy with my brand-new crayons, determined to use all of my colors that same day, when I felt a light tap on my shoulder. I looked up and turned my head slightly. It was Fernando, a classmate. My little heart was filled with tenderness as I looked at his big, brown eyes and shy smile.

"Hi, Clara," he said, his voice so low. It faded before he even finished the sentence, such was his nervousness.

"Hi, Fe," I replied, giving him an encouraging smile.

"I..." Long silence. And then, shaking his head as if to shake the fear away, he continued, "I was at the playground and I found something I wanted to give you."

Only then did I realize that his hands were hidden behind his body. Slowly, he moved them forward, revealing the gift he carried in his trembling fingers: a small flower with red petals. I picked it up carefully, setting the crayons and book aside. I felt my cheeks burn, very aware of the feeling I had, though I couldn't name it. It was the first time I remember losing my words, which were now all incoherent up in my head. I looked away from the flower to Fernando, whose eyes were downcast, and whose face was slightly flushed. Without thinking too much, or understanding clearly the impulse that took hold of me, I went to him and kissed him on the lips.

It is difficult to describe that moment, since there were a thousand sensations at once, all showing themselves to me for the first time. The kiss itself, a little touch of the lips, didn't last more than half a second, but it felt like an infinite time. My whole body felt hot and cold. I was sweating and shivering—a pang of weird guilt, shame, and a "good thing" all mixed together. Fernando looked surprised and unsettled, as I did, not knowing what to do with that explosion of new feelings. When I came back to my senses, I ran away, leaving my crayons, my coloring book, and my little friend behind. I still had in my hand the red flower he had given me.

The memory faded and I returned to the park, to the petal, to the sun, to the solitude. This last one felt like a heavy burden at that moment. I wished Fernando was there with me, no matter how absurd the thought was. I put the flower petal inside my book, and after a few more seconds of daydreaming, I decided to go home. On the subway, while a guy was singing and playing the guitar, I couldn't concentrate on anything other than that feeling. It was a kind of emptiness, somewhat harrowing, but at the same time exciting, full of possibilities. As I rummaged through my purse for coins for the musician, I thought once more about my first kiss. And for the first time in a long time, I also remembered what I did after it happened.

We would have art class after recess. Still overwhelmed by the recent events, I only realized I no longer had my art supplies when the teacher asked us to draw and color something that made us happy. I panicked when I found myself without my crayons. But how to explain to an adult, an authority figure, that I left them behind after venturing to kiss a boy on the mouth? No, I was ashamed of even thinking about it. I looked around my things and found only a pencil and an eraser. I took the pencil, not sure of what I was going to do. On the paper that rested on my desk, infinite possibilities. Timidly, I brought the pencil to the paper, using its gray lead to try to express some happiness. A lot of moments of my then short life made me happy, but I couldn't think of any of them. At least nothing before that last hour. I ended up letting the pencil dance on the piece of paper, leading it almost unconsciously. When I finished, there was the flower that, although gray on the surface, exuded its reddish passion.

The subway conductor's voice woke me up; we had arrived at my station. I got off the train and went up the stairs. When I got to the street, I realized it was dark. The sun went down very early in the winter. In the apartment, there was a note from my roommate, saying she would be staying at her boyfriend's house. Well, he wasn't really her "boyfriend," but they spent so much time together that they could be mistaken for a committed couple. I opened the fridge and found the leftover pizza we'd ordered the night before. Pepperoni. I missed the Portuguese pizza from São Paulo. I put it on a paper towel and warmed it up in the microwave, my mind still going back to my childhood. After that day, the flower, the kiss, I continued to draw. Everything I saw, felt, and imagined, I could turn into something tangible on any piece of paper. In fact, on any surface. I went from paper to canvases, walls, even faces when I discovered makeup.

As I ate my slice of pizza, I wondered what had happened that made me stop. I concluded that it was just life, pure and simple. When you have to worry about graduating from college, working, and paying bills, the days get shorter and shorter. Our "free" time is also for work—to forget about it, to rest from it. Maybe I should go back to art. After all, my classes would soon start, and my hours would be taken away once more.

When I finished eating, I went into my room in search of something that could be my blank canvas.

I found among my papers a draft of the university application. I put it down on my study desk, clearing the mess around it, and leaving the clean page facing up. Within my reach, at that moment, I found a black pen and a green highlighter. I picked up the pen, and as it touched the paper, an old feeling came back to me. Actually, in reality, I think it had been there the whole time, only asleep. I felt it awakening with every stroke, every shape and shading. Part of me wanted to laugh with happiness, and another part was barely aware of my existence. I was a mere instrument of that art; I didn't matter. My name, my face meant nothing. When I finished, I was overcome with exhaustion.

I woke up in the middle of the night, my face crumpled over my drawing. The paper now had the marks of the slight deformity that my face, heavy with sudden sleep, had given it. But it took me a few seconds to realize—that I'd fallen asleep right there at the table. I turned off the light, still surrounded by the almost drunken confusion of somnolence's nature. I went to bed and almost immediately fell asleep again.

The next day, I felt a lone ray of sunlight coming through the window and landing on my face, waking me up. I was overly rested. I stretched slowly, and only then did I check the time on my phone—a startle: I was late for work. I got up, brushed my teeth, grabbed my backpack, and ran out. The diner I worked at was only three blocks away, and I was able to arrive just in time to open. Triumph!

My boss, who was unlocking the door, glared at me.

"I'm so sorry, Mr. Alexander, my alarm clock didn't go off."

The old man muttered something in Greek, his native language, and gestured with his hand for me to hurry up and get to work. I ran to the bathroom and put on my uniform. That day, customers seemed fussier and more demanding, and my shift (which lasted breakfast and lunch) seemed to fly by. I barely had time to stop and eat. I served elaborate, delicious meals all morning, and all I ate was a muffin.

I'm not sure if it was the rush of work, the fact that I didn't eat much, or the energy spent the night before, but all I wanted when I left the diner was to take a nap. I dragged myself back to the house, threw my things on the living room floor, and lay down on the sofa. I fell into a wonderful dream, in which colors rained as if the rainbow had shattered in the sky and fallen to the earth. I wasn't in New York, but in the backyard of my childhood home in São Paulo. The collapsing drops of color painted every part of the moldy wall, the rusty gate, and the uneven floor. I, too, was nothing more than a mixture of pigments and shades.

I woke up to the sound of the door lock. It was Kat, my roommate.

"Hey, sorry, I didn't mean to wake you up," she said, noticing my confused awakening.

"No problem," I replied. "I've probably overslept, anyway. How was it at Jordan's?"

"Oh, the usual, you know."

I didn't know. But I nodded as if I understood.

"And how was work?" she asked.

"Busy."

I sat up, yawning, trying to find some energy to get through the rest of the day that would drag on for quite a few hours. She went to her room, and I took the opportunity to turn on the TV. A chocolate commercial had my mind racing with hunger. My body agreed in tune, making my stomach grumble in an animal growl.

"Kat!" I yelled. "Are you hungry? I think I'll order Chinese food."

She left her room, a little embarrassed smile on her face. "Mmm... Clara, can I steal a tampon?"

"Sure. They're in my bedside table drawer."

"Thanks."

As she headed to my room, I took the menu of a Chinese restaurant. The food wasn't the best in the world, but it was cheaper, and I craved its so-so flavors. Sometimes, that was enough. Before I could decide what to order, though, Kat returned, a tampon in one hand and a sheet of paper in the other. It was my drawing. She looked at it, and at me—an unreadable expression on her face.

"Clara," she said finally, after long seconds, "did you do that?"

She turned the drawing towards me. It was the park with its dead trees and dry grass and its calm. The lake, still frozen, was also portrayed there. But that was just the background. In the foreground, a little girl was holding a flower, eyes closed, seeming to smell its scent.

"Yes, I drew it last night."

Kat looked very impressed, as if in those weeks we'd been living together, she'd never really known me until now.

"I didn't know you were so talented!"

"Oh, I... I don't..."

"You should post this drawing!"

I was confused for a moment.

"What?"

She made a gesture asking me to wait, ran to her room, and, after a few minutes, came back, still holding my drawing, and also her camera. Kat was a photographer.

"What are you...?" I started to ask, but she silenced me with a hand gesture.

She opened the living room window and placed the paper—crumpled but nevertheless pleasant to look at, it wasn't sad—on a little table just below her. She positioned it a few times, and, when satisfied, adjusted the camera to the light and took some pictures.

"Here, take a look." She then showed me the photographs on the camera's screen. And my reaction was the thinking of how art within art made sense. The captured images were so beautiful...!

"I'll send them to you via email. You should post them somewhere."

With that, my roommate went back to her things, leaving me there with myself, as if it was nothing what she had given me—to feel, to think of. I took the drawing from the table, put it back in my room. I looked at it for a long time. I was proud of it—I only realized it now. I wonder why?

New email notification on my phone. It was Kat's pictures.

I unpretentiously turned on my laptop, just because I wanted to see the photos in full size—that was the speech I gave myself. On the computer screen, they were even more magnificent. 'Why not?' I thought. I opened one of my social media profiles, uploaded one of the images, but when I went to click "share," I couldn't do it. I was uncomfortable exposing myself to those people. I wasn't sure why. I just didn't want to be vulnerable to old schoolmates, ex-boyfriends, cousins, friends. I closed that page, opened a search engine, looked for a blog provider, and created one with an email account that didn't have my name in it. I chose a simple design and gave myself the alias black_rose. No hidden meanings, it was just the first name that popped into my head when looking at the black ink flower I had created in the center of my drawing.

I uploaded the image and posted it without captions or anything. I didn't quite know why I was doing it. Did anyone still read blogs these days? Maybe that's why I chose that platform. I don't know. I closed the laptop, went on to order my food. But I couldn't put aside certain unease. My thoughts went as far away as they could. What if no one saw my drawing? What if someone saw it? It certainly didn't matter; my practical side knew it. After all, what did I expect? An art critic finding my work in the infinity of the internet? I laughed at myself when I realized that, behind all the rationality that shaped my thoughts, part of me, in fact, expected precisely the absurdity of that.

⇥⇤

A few days passed, which I filled with concerns about the classes that would soon start. I needed to get used to the American education system, choose classes, start thinking about my thesis, blah, blah, blah—a breakout in the solidity of my mind. My friends laughed when I said I would apply for a Master's in Human Resource Management and Development. My major was in Design, but all I did with it were logos and wedding invitations. It was all right. At least I felt like I was in my "field," being creative and artistic and all. That's what I used to tell myself. But the money I was making wasn't worth putting aside my dream, even though the work brought me a slight feeling of being "where I wanted to be."

One night, while browsing the university's website, I received a new email notification. It was from my blog server. Honestly, I had even forgot-

15

ten about that rush of spontaneity. I thought the message must be something reminding me to post more; the best idea would be to delete the whole thing. However, to my complete surprise, the email informed me of a new comment. An irrefutable, unsuspected curiosity. I went to my page with the agility that only urgency accesses. The single comment on my post was made by a Dark Angel. What a cliché! Here's what it said:

"I saw myself in your drawing. Keep making art."

The fact that something so concise made me smile spontaneously disconcerted me. Then, some stranger among millions of IPs, saw my art. Not only did they see it, they understood and liked what I expressed. I spent several seconds looking at the computer screen, rereading that little sentence, a few words that, although I didn't know it yet, would be the beginning of my sense of self for a long time. Finally, I clicked on "reply." I wasn't very good with words and I don't think I'd have the right ones anyway, but I gave it a try.

"Thank you for telling me that. I will."

I sent it, and immediately afterward, forgetting that I was supposed to think about school, I closed my laptop and opened my drawer in search of a sheet of paper. Without thinking too much, just letting the shapes flow from my hand, I started becoming aware of the images that appeared on the paper. I used colors this time. Simple crayons that I took with me when I babysat. The landscape was made of sand dunes, and in the background, the sun was setting, orange, the color mixing with the beige of the grains that made up the hills, making the image light up. The sea was close, it was known, although it was not shown in that composition.

When satisfied with my work, I spent some time contemplating it. Appreciation without ambition. Then I took a picture of it with my cell phone camera. And I posted it on the blog right away. This time with the caption "Light." After that, I couldn't concentrate on anything, neither trifles nor important matters. Nothing but art itself, and its fruits. Secretly, in a place in my brain where I kept the inconsistencies that I wanted to hide from myself, I waited for Dark Angel to see my new drawing and leave another comment. My thoughts flew away, although I tried to suppress them with the logic of reason. Once again, of course, it (reason) lost the internal battle.

No longer able to think about anything that was tangibly and legitimately real, I decided to clean up my room a little—I cleaned when I felt overwhelmed. And so I did. Low music, worn-out clothes... While dusting the furniture, sweeping, or folding clothes, I couldn't ignore the metaphor that was present. But when was life not metaphorical? Get rid of the dirt, the mess, let it all flow perfectly, until, without my noticing it, sneaky and silent, the filth took over once again. It was an eternal cycle: clean, dirty, clean...

When I finished, so did the philosophical thoughts. After all, what's the point of agonizing over something that won't change? I don't know how some poor souls do it, whose work consists of that. Philosophers and poets, for example. I myself could barely deal with the occasional ramblings that took over me. But finally putting aside the abstractions, I surrendered to the calmness being there brought me, breathing the sweet chemical aroma of recently applied cleaning products.

I sat in a chair, the music still in the air, a song that reminded me of my country. I took out my cell phone and checked one of my social media accounts. All lives seemed very fulfilled on the screen of the device. Of course, it was foolishness, I knew—that people molded themselves however they wanted in the internet world. 'Not a bad thing,' I thought. Humanity needs an escape, and why not look at yourself in a perfect selfie and inflate your ego with a shower of likes? I wondered, however, what was happening in the context of each of those photos and small motivational texts from my friends. What did that girl really mean when she posted a picture with her boyfriend along with a caption full of sweet words? Perhaps nothing more than what the words said; perhaps the exact opposite.

Again, I had let myself be carried away by these thoughts that didn't belong to me. So I decided to seek distraction with cute, silly videos, which I did for a while. And then, when I checked my email, I got a notification of a new blog comment. My heart, for a second, seemed to both stop and beat harder than ever. When I accessed my page and saw that Dark Angel had written to me again, I felt something in my stomach, a feeling similar to hunger. It wasn't so much a physical hunger, even though it lived deep inside me, but something hard to explain—a desire that wasn't addressed to anything in particular. It was just there, existing, persistent. I went to the comments part of the site and found the message.

"Wow, those colors are intense! I wonder what was going through your mind as you worked on this creation."

Done. The "hunger" had passed. This was what my body craved, this stranger's words. It was a part of me that, once dormant, was now awakening with an almost uncontrollable urge. Urge for what? For being appreciated, understood? For existing through art, even if only for that one person? I'm not sure, but the feeling was enough for me. I didn't need to give it a name or a meaning. And the euphoria fed me. I responded to my Dark Angel.

"I couldn't answer that in a million years. When I'm creating, I can't tell what's going on in my head. Art just...comes."

Like a ritual that, even though it had just begun, felt like part of a tradition that lasted for lifetimes, I felt the urge to draw once more. In those last days, that pulse has lived in every muscle of my body and I couldn't imagine how I had gone so many years without feeling it. It was the reason for everything when I let it flow; it was the root of my existence.

In automatic movements, I reached for a sheet of paper in my drawer and, again, used crayons for my composition. Different shades of blue and green now took over the paper, forming, in the end, the vision of the calm sea. The sky was sheltered by a few white clouds and a small sailing boat could be seen along the horizon line. I took a picture of my work, once again following the rite, but I didn't post it on the blog right away this time. I wanted Dark Angel to sleep with the fresh feeling of my other drawing still in their mind.

I felt exhausted once again. All this commotion inside of me was too much to handle. And why? Some children's crayon drawings and concise comments from a random person on a blog. It was absurd that such insignificant things would leave me like this. But they did. It was all right. Between work and college, I soon wouldn't have time to deal with this nonsense. I laughed at myself as I went to bed, thinking about how, as a teenager, I had never been carried away by this sort of thing, and now, as a grown woman, here I was. I fell asleep almost immediately upon lying down, and in the unconsciousness of that brief paralyzed state, everything suddenly lost its importance.

Spring

S pring had arrived, bringing its glorious shapes and colors and smells. The cold was leaving us, the snow was melting, and my soul felt that mild warmth full of expectations. It was my first day of school. The college campus was beautifully adorned by nature, and a mixture of shades covered the grass, which was filled with flowers that fell from the trees. In Brazil, the seasons were not so perfectly separated. It was often eighty degrees in the middle of winter. Here in New York, however, I could clearly see the weather changing—in the landscapes and in people, who also took on more color at that time of the year.

I was early for my first day. It was the same thing the week before, when we had orientation. That was when I understood it would be a much more difficult adaptation than I imagined, even though I had read absolutely everything I could about how American colleges work. It's funny, as much as we know about the universe of differences between theory and practice, how the irrefutability of things surprises us. I woke up very early that morning; anxiety was my alarm clock. I got up, got my books ready, spent a little time doing my makeup... and now there I was, sitting on a bench near the building where my classes would be, enjoying the beautiful view with a giant cup of coffee in my hand. No matter how I always asked for the strongest they had, I ended up getting that watery drink in one of those huge cups, and all I thought about was the strained coffee I drank in Brazil.

As I lost myself in homesickness, I watched the people who passed by occasionally. There weren't that many at that time. Some wore gym clothes and went for a morning run. Others read as they walked, being careful not to bump into a tree or any other distracted person who also had their face in a book. Others walked in a hurry, carrying their backpacks and drinking their giant coffees, looking for some energy to start the day.

I checked the clock on my phone. I still had some time before my first class. I suddenly realized I was a little nervous about the whole thing—being in a different system than the one I was used to in Brazil, with classes in a language that wasn't mine and papers and theses and exams and all that. A loose thought in the midst of chaos: Dark Angel. I hadn't posted anything else on the blog since the picture of those dunes. I wondered what he was doing—and if he was thinking of me. And right after that frenzy, I was infuriated by the effect that this person with whom I had exchanged two messages had on me. That was one of the reasons, I think, why I hadn't posted anything else. Yet here he was, uninvited, inhabiting my mind—invading, taking over, propagating.

I shook my head and decided to go to the classroom in an attempt to distract myself from the internal tantrums. Every seat was vacant, of course, and I sat in the corner row, sipping on my coffee—and waiting. Gradually, the chairs were taken by students. People looked at each other shyly for a few seconds. Some muttered "good morning," but for the most part there was no interaction. 'Well, typical first-day-of-school behavior,' I thought. I didn't know that little would change over time. I was the only non-American in the class. The closest to me was a Colombian woman, but she didn't really fit the definition of a foreigner, as she arrived in the United States as a baby. Even so, she was different from the others, raised in America, but with traces of her own heritage at home. Latina, they defined her. And me too.

Elena and I got along from that first day. She was one of the last people to enter the room. She arrived very smiley and excited, shaking her blonde-dyed hair as she looked around, blatantly watching each of her classmates. They were very disconcerted by that shameless woman. As she turned to face me, I smiled back, not immediately looking away like the others. She shook her head slightly, sat down next to me. Speaking loudly, with a slight Hispanic accent, she introduced herself.

"Good morning! My name is Elena."

I replied as kindly as I could. "Good morning! Nice to meet you, Elena, I'm Clara."

She observed me without subtlety, and I took the opportunity to do the same to her. Elena was older, in her early forties, with a family and children, as I discovered later. She had brown eyes that were very curious and wide-open, not afraid of being read. Her face was covered in heavy makeup, and red lipstick was her most striking feature. She was the opposite of what was expected of a graduate student at a reputable university. And her honest presence bothered the others, one could see. No one was used to living with such blatant truths.

"Where's that accent from?" she asked.

"Brazil. São Paulo."

"Wow, how wonderful, Clara!" She pronounced my name without that American accent; she was the only one who did it.

Before I could answer her, however, the teacher entered the classroom. The next few hours were filled with the basics of managing people, with no other voice present but that of Mr. Clark. I had learned that we don't call professors "teacher," as we do in Brazil, but, respectfully, by their surname (or first name, if they were younger).

My notes, between yawns, took over the notebook pages, so disorganized they could be mistaken for drafts of children starting to learn how to write. Mr. Clark spoke slowly and boringly, so it was easy to get lost in thoughts that had nothing to do with people management. My drafts turned to sketches of random objects. I drew a turtle with a tired expression, a piano with missing keys, an open book with crumpled pages... By summertime, my notebook would have more pictures than words. Still, I didn't do poorly on the course—nevertheless.

After the first week, I got more or less used to the new routine. Like any good worker, I learned to optimize my time, reading on the subway and during breaks from work, for example. The truth is, I barely had time to think about anything but school. Even in my sleep, I ended up seeing the class slides dance before my eyes, mixed with my messy notes and a thesis made entirely of illustrations. This recurring dream would always wake me up in the middle of the night, and it was nearly impossible to get back to sleep, so I was usually on my cell phone. More than once, I went to my blog page and reread Dark Angel's comments.

I felt more alone every day, even surrounded by people at school and work and in the crowded streets of the city. Elena and I talked quite a lot; however, at the end of classes, she would go home to her family. There were the diner girls, too, but, just like it was with my roommate, our relationships didn't go far beyond the cordiality expected of working together. And because of my classes, I didn't have time to work as a babysitter anymore, and the feeling of emptiness and loneliness stabbed me even harder without the sweet and absurdly honest relationships that children give us.

Because of this feeling, which I saw growing in the face of my impotence, a constant anguish took over me, especially on the rare occasions when I was not busy with school or work. Video calls with my family and friends in Brazil, less and less frequent due to my lack of time, gave me some relief, but it was temporary, and when we said goodbye, the affliction returned with even more intensity. I ended up surrendering to the only thing that calmed my heart a little and went back to posting on the blog. I published, on one of those sleepless nights, the drawing of the lonely boat in the blue-green sea. Only two nights after that, which I spent in the most absolute expectation, already with some hopelessness, to receive a message from him, I saw his comment that, even before being read, warmed me. I ran my eyes over his words.

"I thought I wouldn't see your drawings anymore. I'm glad to know you haven't stopped making art. This boat... is it lost? Or maybe it's just part of the immensity of water that surrounds it. Or perhaps it craves to be. Well, I'm just rambling. I can't wait for the next post."

Just a few lines of remote considerations about my drawing, and the void was filled with egocentric pleasure. He knew how to use words, a strong weapon in the virtual world, and I took advantage of that power as much as he probably did to feed my ego. But the strange thing: despite the circumstances, I trusted him. I felt the truth in his speech, so little, unpretentious. Despite existing in a parallel world, easily manipulated, invented, his words came to me with almost naive sincerity. I ended up finally answering him.

"Maybe the destination of the boat is not important. If it's lost, too, perhaps it doesn't matter. Maybe what matters is the simple fact that it exists."

As soon as I clicked "send," I instantly regretted it. The typed words seemed too pretentious. It felt like I was trying too hard. Trying what? To delve into my own work—the thing that was completely impossible for me. What artist, what creator, can dare to have any consideration about their work? What mind, in any place or time, could dare to judge its own creation? Fools, the ones who try...

In any case, for better or worse, I didn't delete my answer. And eventually, it would arrive at some screen, and enter his eyes. And he would react. Maybe he would smile as he read it; perhaps he would disdain; perhaps he would enjoy it. His fingers would then, in an uncontrollable rush, type out a new message, and our words, though open to anyone who wanted to see them, would reach each other like a whisper that tells an impossible secret.

My thoughts had a life of their own, racing across the surface of my spirit. That was until my heart skipped a beat. Dark Angel had answered me again! This time, the notification sound gave me a different feeling. After all, he was talking to me at that moment. Instantaneous. Brutal. He was awake somewhere, his thoughts attuned to mine. Surreal feeling, of not knowing what, how, why. I opened the page that contained his message. It was actually an answer to mine.

"You're right. What matters is the existence of the boat and what it brings to those who see it."

No more thinking for me. I continued the conversation. I wanted him to know that I was there, awake too, alive, breathing new air, living that moment with him, even if in an artificial way.

"What does the boat bring you, then?"

I waited anxiously, hoping he was feeling something similar to what I was experiencing. What a connection! It'd been a while since I'd experienced this with anyone. I hadn't felt so childish in a while either. It was similar to the feeling of when I was a kid and, in the middle of recess, had my first kiss.

Except, now I was an adult, fully, cruelly aware of my immature, simple-minded... silly feelings. Before I could ponder further, however, I received his reply.

"There aren't enough characters here for me to explain. Want to chat via email?"

I was a little confused for a moment. Chat via email? Why not instant messaging? Texting? DM? Had Dark Angel lived many more years than I had? Did he write letters, send telegrams? Until then, I hadn't given much thought to the human being behind those messages. I thought of them as a "him," but that's all. Our brief conversations, to me, were a bit like prayers, where you don't address a specific someone—at best, a vague image similar to the ones that adorn churches or temples. Well, the truth is, it didn't really matter who the fingers typing on the other side of the screen belonged to. And I ended up convincing myself that I had nothing to lose, which was an invariable truth, given the circumstances. Finally, then, I answered him.

"Sure, why not?"

I also wrote my email address in the message and waited. I closed my eyes briefly, putting the phone aside, and tried to clear my thoughts for a moment. My head took a trip to the past, connected it with the present, guessed the future—an apartment somewhere in the world, decorated with art. I would make a room into an art studio and keep the curtains closed to embrace the obscurity and paint my canvases. Then I would drink wine and read or watch TV. Perhaps. Maybe instead I'd wear formal clothes and work in an office, drinking coffee and reading the newspaper. No, no one else will read printed newspapers in this future of mine. Surely there would be a husband and a dog or a baby there. And the babysitter would come every Saturday night so I could go out to dinner with my man. But I couldn't see his face, even though I knew I got married because he made me laugh and think and discover things. We drove through the city streets, surrounded by lights. He drove. We listened to the radio, but I didn't know any of those songs. What I had left was the pleasure that coursed through my entire being—so unbearably intense that I laughed until I started coughing. Until I almost threw up. The cycle formed and I couldn't control it. When I was gripped by an intensity too violent for the human I am, I woke up alarmed by the sudden confusion that comes with the lucidity that follows dreams.

⚜

I t was still dark outside. The clock displayed four in the morning. It took me a few seconds to sort my thoughts. My neck hurt. I got up and, in the movement, dropped my cell phone on the floor. Then, a sudden anguish came over me when I remembered Dark Angel. Or had I dreamed it too? I checked my phone, and there it was, along with some emails promoting products I didn't need, a message from him. The subject was just "Boat."

"Hello, Black Rose!

As I said before, I'm glad you're back to posting your drawings. I'm not the type of guy who spends that much time on the internet, and while doing a search, I came across your blog by accident. Well, I don't know if it was by accident. Fate, perhaps? Whatever you want to call it. Looking at your drawings, I feel we have something in common, although I can't quite explain what.

Well, you asked me what the boat in your last post brings me. First, it made me think of loneliness. After all, it's just a small boat in an immensity of water. And I also thought that it might be lost. But then I realized that it is part of that place, as much as the sea and the sky that are there. It is not alone or lost, it is just being, existing. Of course, it was you who helped me see such obviousness.

I really hope I see more of your art very soon, and who knows, we can maybe have more conversations about it. Or about anything else; the world is very vast. As just another bored American, I was glad to have found you. I eagerly await your reply.

Dark Angel"

I woke up completely while reading his email. Like a child opening a Christmas present, I felt that little warmth in my chest and smiled, even though I consciously tried to force myself not to. I still resisted, because logic wouldn't leave me alone to enjoy the good feeling. Logic told me that it wasn't normal for a grown woman to be up at four in the morning reading a message from a stranger and feeling such enthusiasm. The intensity of those feelings inside me was much higher than it should be. Even so, as these thoughts rose like a loud, irritating alarm bellowing in my head, with almost automatic gestures, I tapped the "answer" button. Challenging myself, almost like a child throwing a tantrum, I typed out the words I would send next.

"Dark Angel,

You really know how to use words. I wish I had that gift, but I'm afraid I won't have as many interesting things to say. In fact, I never thought I would discuss the hidden meanings of my scribbles on the internet. But I'm glad we're doing it.

I've never met anyone who was so sensitive to art. It's nice to have someone I can talk to about this. Overall, it's hard to find other connoisseurs here in the US. I hope we do keep talking to each other, whether it's about drawings or anything else.

Black Rose"

I couldn't go back to sleep, so I decided to get up and make myself some coffee while trying to sort my mind. In a few hours I would have class, then go to work and then home again. This cycle depressed me. I began to think about what I would do after graduating—a thought that invariably haunted me from time to time. The plans were always to return to Brazil with this diploma, get a good job, earn a lot of money, blah, blah, blah. But now I had my doubts. Some days I would wake up with the almost uncontrollable desire to catch the first plane back to my country and lie in my room at my mother's house and smell her fresh homemade food. On others, however, I felt that my home was in this place that was becoming less and less strange each day, with this language that was beginning to take root in me, shuffling with Portuguese inside my head.

The smell of coffee permeated the air in the kitchen, momentarily pulling me away from my thoughts. I decided it was silly to worry so far in advance. I had two years to think about the after. For now, I allowed myself to enjoy the slightly bitter taste of my coffee and focused on the near future: the test I would have in a few days, Kat's birthday coming up soon, the stain I needed to clean off my work uniform... work. Should I have just continued babysitting? I made more money waiting tables, but also had more headaches. Just the day before, there was that customer with a very strong Indian accent. I got his order wrong. He lost his cool, made a scene, and left me a two percent tip. My boss wasn't happy either. I didn't understand his Greek words, but he made himself understood in such a way that formal language would almost get in the way.

As my mind returned to these unavoidable worries and my coffee cup slowly emptied, I heard a familiar sound from outside. A light rain was pouring over the city. I went to the window. The streets below were already filled with cars and pedestrians, even at that early hour, being bathed in the drops of spring. Colorful umbrellas were spread out on the sidewalks; people were running for cover or getting inside yellow taxis. It was a mini chaos amidst the calmness of the rainy morning. It reminded me of São Paulo with its eternal drizzle and its people always in a hurry.

I finished the last sips of my coffee and went to take a shower. I let myself be for a while. Kat wasn't going to use the shower today, so I enjoyed the massage of the droplets over my body without the constant fear of running out of hot water. My roommate found my habit of showering every day very strange, especially in the winter. I needed to think about her birthday present. We were having a small party at the apartment, and she had asked me to prepare *caipirinhas* for the guests. Kat loved everything "exotic" I brought from Brazil. I can say she was disappointed when I told her that I used the subway in my home country, and not a canoe to get around. I laughed to myself remembering her first questions: "do you have text messages over there'" "was your house near the Amazon;" "you don't speak Spanish in Brazil." I didn't blame her. I'm sure I would ask stupid questions like these to someone from Asia or Africa. The Earth, though immense in extent, seemed to exist only in Europe and the United States.

I finished my long shower, feeling refreshed. It was still raining outside. With the towel wrapped around my hair and wearing a robe, I put my umbrella next to my college stuff. As I was deciding what to wear, my cell phone beeped, the notification sound of a new email. Heart racing slightly, I took the device and saw that Dark Angel had answered me.

"Black Rose,
You certainly woke up early today! I was happy to read your email first thing in the morning. It put me in a good mood to go on with the day. I hope you are also excited for the journey.

You talked about the gift of using words. I don't know if I really have it, but know this: I would trade it for your gift without a second thought. Sometimes we can express so much more with images than with words.

Anyway, I want to see more of your drawings! Have a nice day, and I don't know what the weather is like where you are, but if it's raining, stay dry.
Dark Angel"

A slight shiver ran through me: was he in New York too? No, it was certainly raining elsewhere in the US at that time. Maybe... and the infinite possibilities gave me a strange sensation. Excitement and fear mixed in my mind, in my body. No, I couldn't want to know where he was. I liked the mystery. Dark Angel could be whoever I wanted him to be. In my fantasies, he was a young man with a significant job, like a social worker or a teacher. He was alone, but by choice. He enjoyed his own company. And he had such an absurd intensity that people could barely be in his presence without getting lost in themselves.

I decided to answer him later after I got back from work. That would give me time to calm my anxieties. Even if he was actually very close to me, that didn't matter at all. I thought that, the moment he became a person, with a face and a name, the enchantment would be gone. The infinite possibilities would no longer exist, and I would have to accept whatever he was. I realized right away that this scenario was not what I wanted. The best would be to keep the enigma of his existence. No matter what, we would always have these invisible beings on the internet to talk to. Yes, I was invisible too, at the mercy of his imagination.

The rain got a little stronger and woke me up to the day that claimed my attention. I got dressed, went out into the gray streets crowded with people fleeing nature, and did, once again, what I had taken on as a duty for another day of learning. The floor near the classroom door accommodated a small puddle of water, formed by the droplets that fell from the arriving students. Raincoats, rain boots, and umbrellas joined us that day, and the gray of the weather suddenly turned into a mixture of colors and patterns so diverse they looked like part of an abstract painting. I smiled at the insistence of joy imposing itself on that rainy day.

When the first class's teacher began to speak, we could barely hear her, such was the vigor that the storm was now showing. She finally gave up and directed us to read a chapter from that semester's textbook. I tried to focus on the chapter about work safety, but the sound of falling water distracted me. After reading the same sentence three times, I gave up and let my eyes see only random letters on those pages. I looked from the book to the teacher, who was reading, too, but from something that seemed to have nothing to do with the class. I could see through her dreamy eyes. Then I let my gaze wander around the room, finding sleepy, bored faces glued to their books. Well, not all. Some people were looking at their phones, and a guy opened a comic book. My eyes continued to roam around the room when, suddenly, they were surprised by another pair that looked at me with curiosity.

I turned my head away, facing my book of nonsense words again. From across the room, I could see in my peripheral vision that he was still watching me. I didn't know his name. He was quiet, even more so than the rest of the students. So quiet that I hadn't noticed him until a week into the course, and only because he'd chosen to sit right next to me on that occasion. He must have been around thirty years old, light-brown hair, bright-blue eyes. His features were strong, serious. He looked like he was always angry. He didn't speak to anyone. In fact, I had never heard his voice. His hair was soaking wet that day, thanks to the rain. A leather jacket hung over the back of his chair, and the white T-shirt he wore was also wet.

For the rest of the class, I forced myself to read that chapter of the textbook, and it was a huge effort to keep my eyes glued to those pages. I still felt that stranger watching me, and the sensation was uncomfortable. He could find out a thousand things about me, and there was nothing I could do to keep my secrets intact. My body expression, my clothes, my skin that I knew to be flushed would give them away to that man. I hated him for stripping me so blatantly, taking me out of the comfort of invisibility I often placed myself in.

W hen the class finally ended, the rain already easing, I sighed in relief and went out into the hallway to stretch my legs and get away from the situation. I ended up heading to the bathroom, where I washed my face, fixed my hair, and took a few breaths in front of the mirror. My cheeks were, as I'd imagined, slightly pink. At that moment, Elena, my classmate, came out of one of the toilet stalls. Seeing me, she smiled happily and, with her characteristic lack of discretion and clear inefficiency at detecting contexts, she abruptly asked, "So, Clara, how's your love life going? Are you going out with anyone?"

The sudden question left me a little disconcerted for a moment. She always asked that kind of thing or made casual comments at random times (or maybe they weren't that random). Over time, I got used to it, but on that day, my emotions were a little too much to handle.

"Oh...no, I haven't dated anyone since I've moved here."

Saying that aloud, I realized what a fiasco my social life had become. It had been forever since I went to a bar or club, to dance, to see people. I was either too busy or too tired for that. Kat would sometimes invite me to hang out with her and meet her friends, but for one reason or another,

I never did. And this inertia toward having relation-ships existed even before I moved to the USA. With the insane preparations for the trip, the preceding months were all for suitcases, documents, visa, bu-reaucracy...

"Mmm," Elena said again, snapping me out of my reverie. "I noticed John was looking at you today. He's very cute, don't you think? If I was younger and single..."

And the blonde burst out laughing as if she was a teenager. I laughed with her, amused by her enthu-siasm, but a little distressed. She also noticed that he was watching me. Yes, John was his name. Now I remembered. And indeed, he was a very attractive man. However, I didn't necessarily think that the fact he looked at me that morning had anything to do with flirtation or intentions, the passionate lyri-cism that begins with the infamous first exchange of glances.

"Don't be silly," I replied. "He was just bored."

She, who was touching up her red lipstick, sud-denly stopped, looking at me with her typical sassi-ness.

"I was bored, too, so I decided to kill time by looking at the most handsome guy in the room. That's when I noticed he was doing the same thing. Well, with the prettiest girl, of course."

She giggled one more time and winked at me before going back to applying her lipstick. I smiled at her amusement without saying anything else. John never spoke to anyone. But if he wanted to ask me out, I would gladly accept. In addition to the classic handsomeness that fits anyone's standards, his mystery was fascinating. Impossible to read him, different from almost anyone else, and not just because of his silence. His grave features allowed for a range of possibilities. Maybe he was just grumpy, but who knows? Perhaps that was just a facade—to hide what? I wondered what his smile looked like, that is if anything could make him smile. And if so, what?

Elena was leaving the bathroom now, and I followed her. The next class would soon begin. This time, luckily, we would probably have a regular class with the professor giving his talk, and I could just concentrate on the course. Through the window, I saw that the rain had turned into a light drizzle. The windows were fogged up from the inside, and outside, drops fell lightly, trailing down and finally disappearing like hard tears that fade on the sad faces of disillusioned souls.

As soon as I sat down, I couldn't resist the urge to look at where John was. He was reading now, a thick book, but I couldn't see the title. I then looked at Elena, who was smiling, looking at me with her familiar amused expression. I laughed at her and nodded, then turned my attention once more to my fascinating classmate. He was looking at his book with passion, which was reflected in his gaze very clearly, although his facial expression had barely changed. I heard the professor's footsteps coming to the door, but before I could turn around or do anything, in an instant, John turned and looked directly at me. I felt as if I had been caught in some shameful act. The whole thing only lasted a few seconds, but it felt excruciatingly long.

This time, I couldn't look away as quickly as I would've liked. He also held his gaze, and we only moved our eyes away when the teacher's footsteps reached the front of the room and he started the class. John began to pay attention to the professor's speech, closing his book and putting it in his backpack, but I couldn't concentrate very much. It had been a while since I had reacted to a presence with such enthusiasm. It was a contraction in my stomach and a tingling in my legs—an eagerness I hadn't felt in a long time. I also felt that whatever was going on inside me was reciprocated. His eyes had something voracious that proved that theory.

For the entire rest of the school day, it was like this: eyes crossing and small internal bodily explosions. How had I not noticed such connectivity before? How had I not even noticed his presence for so long? Now it was impossible for me to remain oblivious to him.

At the end of the last class, while packing my things, I checked my phone, which had been off until then, and saw that I had received an email from Dark Angel. It was as if all my senses, which were already in an uproar that day, heightened even more. As I was about to open the message, I felt a presence beside me. I raised my head slightly and saw John, who was looking in my direction as if expecting something from me. He didn't say anything for a few seconds, and we just stood there, staring at each other as we had that morning, with the difference that he was now dangerously close. Those outbursts, the excitement, returned immediately.

Finally, convinced that I would not be the one to break the silence, he said, with some hesitation, "Hi, I... I'm John." He smiled sheepishly. So there it was, his smile. Although clumsy, it was contagious. I couldn't stop my own lips from opening in an expression of amusement.

"Hi, I'm Clara," I replied, putting my phone aside, almost forgetting that I was very anxious to read the message from my virtual friend.

"Yeah, I know. You are the Brazilian girl, right?"

"Yes, that's me."

He looked a little more comfortable now, and his smile became more natural, wider.

"I was thinking," he continued, "would you like to get some coffee one of these days?"

I'm not sure, but I believe my countenance had brightened. Not bad for a rainy day with no prospects. I replied, in a smiling voice, "I would love to. In fact, I still have a few hours before I have to go to work if you're free now..."

"Yes, I am. There's a great coffee place two blocks from here."

"Perfect."

I grabbed my things, put my phone in my bag, not even thinking about Dark Angel anymore, and walked with him. The rain had completely stopped now and a shy sun graced us with its presence. I thought, with euphoria, that somewhere there was a rainbow brightening someone's day. I couldn't think of anything that the arch of colors in the sky couldn't make better.

As we walked, we talked a little about the day's classes, the weather, the small trivialities of life. I realized then and there that he was one of those people who needed to fill the silence some-how—not talking was certainly uncomfortable for him. I also noticed that he kept a certain distance from me, making sure that even our arms didn't touch. I couldn't help but compare the behavior to that of Brazilian men as I recalled the experiences I'd had with my romantic interests back home.

I noticed things while we walked; that his voice was deep, matching his features—his manner of speaking was slow, unhurried. That he became less nervous each time I nodded approvingly at anything he had said or when I smiled at him with interest. That his speech eased a little. At times, it felt like we were old friends. In other times, however, he retreated again, as if suddenly remembering the context of our interaction.

We finally arrived at the coffee house he had suggested. It was a small, cozy place with posters of 1980s rock bands hanging on the walls and jazz music playing softly in the background. There were half a dozen people there. Certainly, the place was frequented by locals for the facade was so discreet that it almost went unnoticed by passers-by in the busy New York City. They preferred the franchised type of place found on every corner.

We sat at a corner table overlooking a small window. We could see an alley outside, with a garbage can, a stray cat roaming around, and countless cigarette butts on the floor. As soon as we were seated, a smiling waitress came to take our orders.

"A latte, please, with skim milk," John asked in an almost solemn voice.

The girl made a note in her notebook, and I found it all extremely quaint and retro. In the diner I worked at, we took the customer's orders on a tablet. She then looked at me, waiting.

"A medium black coffee with two shots of espresso, please."

She went back to writing in her notebook.

"Cream, milk?" she asked in a sweet voice.

"No thanks, just sweetener."

I still hadn't gotten used to having to explain in such detail how I wanted my drink. In Brazil, you just need to order a coffee and that's it. Coffee with milk or *pingado* is the maximum variation, at least in the delis of Sampa, where gourmet food has not yet arrived. Finally, the waitress left us alone.

"Black coffee, huh?" John commented. Most Americans didn't drink it like that. They found it too bitter.

"Well, I'm Brazilian, remember?"

He smiled tenderly.

"It's true. Best coffee in the world?"

"For sure!"

We were silent for a few moments. He soon broke said silence, though, given his already noted urge to fill in the gaps of stillness.

"And so, Clara, tell me a little bit about yourself."

"Oh, well... I was born and raised in São Paulo, Brazil, graduated from college there, and decided to get my Master's abroad. I arrived here a few months ago. I work as a waitress. I think that's it."

He paid immense attention to everything I said. His eyes gleamed with curiosity, almost as if he was facing an exotic animal. Or maybe that comparison isn't fair—who knows?

"You certainly summed up a lifetime very well." A small, wry laugh after the sentence. I couldn't decide whether the sarcasm pleased me or not.

"Well, I'm not very good with words... Why don't you tell me about yourself first?"

The waitress arrived with our beverages. As I put a bag of powdered sweetener into my huge cup, I could feel him watching my movements. The clink of the spoon I used to stir my drink took over our surroundings, almost silencing the music that came from who-knows where. As I lifted my coffee and brought it to my lips, my gaze met his. His latte still lay on the table, untouched. His eyes, once again, made me feel a shiver that ran through my whole body. Even sitting, I noticed that my knees weakened. I put the coffee back on the table, afraid of losing even more control over my own body. For the first time in a long time, I was now the person who was bothered by the silence. I coughed lightly to clear my throat and repeated the question from before. "So? Won't you tell me about yourself?"

He smiled and shook his head slightly as if remembering something.

"Oh, yes, yes, of course... Well, I grew up in upstate New York, in a town near Connecticut. I moved to the city when I was in college and have lived here ever since. My background is in Finance, but I got tired of working so much with numbers and decided I wanted to get more involved with people. So I signed up for our course."

He stopped talking for a moment and took a sip of his drink.

"I work in the finance department of a preschool and teach music as a volunteer at a community center."

"Oh, really? What do you teach?"

"The guitar, basically."

"Interesting... What kind of music do you play?"

"Oh, well, I... I don't really play that well, but I like to play around with jazz, rock, stuff like that... I really like your bossa nova, too."

"Mmm, let me guess... 'The Girl from Ipanema'?"

He chuckled, then had a little more of his latte before answering me.

"Yes, it's a classic."

"It really is."

"And you, what kind of music do you like?"

"Oh, well, everything. It depends on my mood. I really like Brazilian popular music, including 'my bossa nova.' Also jazz and rock, and I enjoy contemporary pop, hip hop... Well, as I said, it depends on my mood."

"And aside from music, what else do you like?"

"Oh, you know, the usual. Movies, TV shows, books, bars..."

"You're not very specific, are you?"

I stopped for a second, sipped my coffee, thought for a moment about what he had said. Was I being too distant? What was I afraid of? Exposing myself? I already felt completely naked with John when he looked at me. What difference would it make sharing such trivial things as my interests and hobbies?

"You're right. Sometimes I can be a little too evasive... Well, let's see. I like horror movies."

"Horror movies?"

"Yes, both bad classic trashy movies with villains that rise from the dead and those new cult movies with a more psychological kind of horror."

"Wow, okay... that's pretty specific."

"I like to read books that are easy to understand. I don't like the ones that make me think too much. I like pizza with coffee in the morning. I prefer beer to any other alcoholic beverage, no matter the circumstances. I hate talking about politics. I hate driving. But I like cars."

I stopped talking to take another sip of coffee and watch John's reaction. He was smiling with his lips and with his eyes, seeming to want to decipher me at all costs. It was clear that part of me was transparent and another part...well, that other part that was a mystery to him wasn't exactly clear to me either.

"You are a very interesting person," he said at last. I wondered if this was a good thing or a bad thing. From his amused expression, I concluded it was good to be interesting.

"You, too."

We stayed there for several more minutes, between conversations, laughter, and small, cozy silences. I almost forgot that I needed to work. When I realized what time it was, I told him I had to run. He left some money on the table and walked me to the subway station. When I got there, I thanked him for the coffee.

"My pleasure."

"See you tomorrow in class?"

"Yeah, sure. Unless..." He paused briefly, looking at me expectantly. "Unless you might want to do something tonight."

I was a little surprised at such spontaneity, given the circumstances—coming from a clearly shy man. Uncontrollable sensations were about to overtake me. Afraid he would notice how irregular my breathing was, I answered him almost in a sigh. "Sure, I would love to."

He then wrote down my phone number in his cell phone contacts, and I headed for the subway platform, still a little stunned, my senses half asleep. Again, I almost forgot I needed to hurry so I wouldn't be late for work. I got on the train still feeling that my legs weren't obeying me as fast as I would have liked. Soft, but hard. Contradictory. And for the rest of the way, I let my mind wander, imagining what my date would be like. It would be my first date with an American. I thought of all the romantic comedies I'd seen but reminded myself that almost none of my real experiences were like what Hollywood had sold me. How many silly dreams they had destroyed. But never mind that. Sometimes reality is even better. Sometimes.

I tried to stop thinking about what it would be like and occupied my head with other things: Kat's birthday, my course final paper, the coffee machine I needed to clean at work... However, those random thoughts didn't return with the firmness of my legs or with the normal beats of my heart, which played its own rhythm, accelerated, oblivious. The images in my mind flashed back to the future; the night that would happen. What would I wear? Would I wait for his call or text all day? I thought I was long past that phase. Apparently, something of the teenage Clara still lingered in me.

⟫⟫⟫ ⟪⟪⟪

I got to work on time, after all. I put my stuff in my locker, not before checking my phone. I expected to see a message from John. However, what I found was Dark Angel's email. I had completely forgotten about my virtual friend. I felt weird...guilty? Guilty. I opened it to read since my shift hadn't started.

"Black Rose,
I passed a graffiti wall on my way to work and thought of you. It was a drawing of a boat. Of course, it didn't have the intensity of your work, but I spent a few seconds watching it. It's been on my path for years, and I just realized its existence today.
Thank you for making me more aware of the art around me.
Dark Angel"

I didn't have time to answer him. I went to work. And for the entire time, it was like I was daydreaming. In my head, fantasies involving John were mixed with others in which Dark Angel and I pursued our artistic aspirations. Listening to customers' orders and taking them, serving tables, cleaning, sweeping floors... all automatic. I lost my notions of reality. My legs and arms moved with agility and my face wore the usual robotic smile as if they were independent from the rest of me. And all through that working day, I felt like a programmed machine.

Finally, at the end of the journey, my body and mind seemed to come back together into a single being—which being that was, I didn't know. I was exhausted. I quickly changed my clothes and grabbed my things from the locker, checking my cell phone again. I saw a message from John.

"Hey, how about Frankie's tonight? Around 9 pm?"

Frankie's was a bar near school. I had never been there, but many classmates went to the place. I responded promptly.

"It's a date. See you later."

Then I reread Dark Angel's email and wrote him back.

"Dark Angel,
I'm glad to hear you found some art on your way.
And that you thought of me.
Black Rose"

⟫⟫ ⟪⟪

When I got home that day, I was still overwhelmed by everything. I went to shower. I had already showered in the morning, but the rain and the work sweat and the need to relax demanded that I did it again. Water was definitely my element. I let the hot drops fall on my head, eyes closed, contemplating the infinite nothingness. I focused only on the pleasant warmth that enveloped my body, and my mind ended up in a meditative state. When I was satisfied and turned off the shower, I felt refreshed, my energies vibrating in harmony.

Towel wrapped around my body, wet hair letting go of small droplets that disappeared over my shoulders, I went to my closet to look for what to wear on the date with John. In general, I didn't spend a lot of time thinking about clothes. I ended up wearing most of the same things (leggings or jeans, a T-shirt and sneakers), but oh, not tonight. I spent a good few minutes looking at what I had—doubts, doubts. Finally, I ended up opting for a dress. It was simple but very pretty with a spring pattern of yellow flowers. I also wore black sandals and a denim jacket over everything. I fixed my hair, did a light makeup... so careful with my appearance that would be a star for a few seconds before the discovery of each other's personalities. I looked at my ready self in the mirror. I liked what I saw.

As I passed the living room, Kat, who was sprawled out on the couch watching a reality show on TV, suddenly got up and looked me up and down.

"Wow, Clara! You look beautiful!"

"Thank you. I kind of have a date."

She smiled, surprised.

"Really? You didn't tell me anything..."

"It happened today. When I arrived, you were in your room. I didn't want to disturb you."

"And who's the guy?"

"He's from college. We had coffee this morning and now we're going to a bar."

She was super excited about the whole thing, one could tell.

"After you get back, I want to know everything! Have fun!"

"I'll tell you all about it. See you later!"

It was still eight o'clock when I left the house. I was anxious—I realized that as I got closer to arriving. As I climbed the stairs of the subway station, I suddenly realized that I was going to live something completely different from what I was used to, which was a paradox of my existence lately. After all, I was starting to get used to new experiences. I thought once more about the familiarity of that culture that I always had, having been born in Brazil. We consume everything American, and we end up thinking that the customs of these people become a little our own—which, in fact, they sometimes do. However, being on this land and experiencing things instead of seeing them on screens brings a new understanding of the world.

I quickly arrived at the bar, which was a couple of blocks from the subway. There were few people there—some tables occupied by groups or couples and a few loners at the bar, watching the football game on TV or chatting with one of the bartenders. The place, like many other bars in that country, resembled an Irish pub: a darker atmosphere, several posters, and trinkets that made references to baseball or football teams and Irish culture. There was a pool table in a corner, where two girls were playing.

I sat at the bar near the entrance, and ordered a beer. The bartender brought me a tall glass filled with my favorite: wheat beer with a slice of orange—something my Brazilian friends would immediately condemn, I'm sure. I took a sip and glanced at my phone. It was still early, eight thirty-five. I stared at the TV, pretending to watch the game and trying to control my nervousness. I'd been trying to understand the rules of this mega-popular sport for some time with no success. Kat had tried to explain it to me a few times, just like baseball, and I understood about sixty percent of it at the time of the explanation, but I always forgot afterward.

Distracted by the TV, and after almost finishing my second glass of beer, I felt a tap on my shoulder. I looked back and saw John, who was smiling shyly. I hugged him and kissed him lightly on the cheek as a greeting, which immediately disconcerted him. I had forgotten that my Brazilian-ness was sometimes too much for the repressed ways of Americans, but at that moment, I didn't really care. Alcohol made me oblivious to these things we tried to repress. He sat next to me, ordered a beer as well—a stronger kind, with a more bitter flavor—and took off his leather jacket (the same one he wore in the morning), revealing a tight black T-shirt. I noticed the muscles in his arms and was a little surprised, as he didn't seem like the type of person who works out, but then I mentally scolded myself for getting caught up in stereotypes.

"So have you been here long?" he asked, snapping me out of my reverie.

"A little, but I left home early," I replied.

"You look beautiful." At this point, John averted his eyes a little from my face. It was funny to be with a shy man. All the other guys I'd dated before were the opposite of that. I smiled and thanked him for the compliment. "Thank you. So do you."

He thanked me, still embarrassed, and got back to his beer. The beginning of our date was like that, full of shy smiles, averted glances, and friendly murmurs—college, work, weather, sports... After a while, and a few glasses of beer, the conversation started to flow better. I discovered that he was a boxer and that he liked to run. He seemed attached to his family and displayed certain tenderness when he told some anecdote involving his mother. He was an only child, he liked dogs, and his favorite holiday was Thanksgiving. I ended up revealing some things about myself, too, a glimpse of how I lived in Brazil, my likes, and even some fears.

I shared trivial family stories with him, compared some of my culture to his, and we both laughed at the ironies and wits of existence.

I'd lost count of how many beers I'd had, but time seemed to pass differently than usual as we talked. Some minutes lasted eternities and others, nothing more than milliseconds. I felt the good warmth of drunkenness take over my body little by little. John seemed quite excited, and I suspected that this state was also a product of alcohol. That evening, I saw him smiling more than in all the time I'd known him. Even more, I saw him laughing, taken by pleasure. When he let go, he left his defenses vulnerably open, and that gave me security.

"So?" I asked at one point. "How different is it to go out with a Brazilian woman?"

"Very," he replied, laughing. "It's a different type of conversation, of course, but besides, you seem warmer, I think. I'm not sure that's the word, but you understand, don't you? I feel warmed up by you, I don't know... there's certain... I don't know."

He started laughing even harder at his own lack of words, and I laughed with him. We ordered another round of beers, and I remembered to check the time. It was eleven-thirty. A small voice inside of my head reminded me that I needed to get up early the next day, but I couldn't bring myself to call it a night.

It'd been a while since I'd had this much fun, and an uncontrollable desire for the hours not to pass was all I allowed myself to feel.

"How about you?" Asked John. "Do you see much difference between going out with an American and a Brazilian?"

His eyes showed genuine curiosity and a twinge of... insecurity? Perhaps. I smiled gently at him.

"Yes, you are completely different. Brazilians are more... daring, let's say. Overall. You Americans are more reserved and, perhaps because of this, more polite, more... gentlemen-like."

He smiled at me again, and for a few moments, we just stared at each other without speaking. The energy around us was very pleasant, a mixture of tenderness and ardor, opposites that complemented each other. John shifted his gaze a little to our surroundings and turned back to me, staring deeply into my eyes.

"Can I kiss you?" he asked then, and I couldn't help but laugh, which made his face break into an apprehensive expression.

"Sorry, I'm not laughing at you. It's just not common to be asked if I can be kissed."

"I didn't know if I could kiss you, let alone in public, in a bar. Some girls don't like that."

As he completed his sentence, I brought one of my hands to his face and caressed him lightly, feeling the softness of his stubble. I approached him slowly. When I was very close, to the point of hearing his breathing getting heavier, I noticed the aroma emanating from him. It was something of a rather rustic softness, difficult to put into words. I took advantage of those moments before the kiss as much as I could: hearts racing, hurried breathing, and the expectation of something that would flavor all those sensations.

Finally, after no longer being able to contain the inevitable moment, we brought our lips together, first with a lightness that bordered on imperceptibility and then letting the kiss deepen until we lost ourselves in that intimate touch. My hand was still exploring his face, and he was holding my waist. We ended the kiss after long minutes and I returned to the real world, or almost, not without a certain dizziness, which wasn't coming from the beer this time.

John looked at me, smiling, and we didn't say anything for a few moments. He took a sip of his drink and then, in a relaxed tone, commented, "So you really don't mind being kissed in public."

"Technically, you were the one who was kissed," I replied and finished the beer in my glass in a few gulps. He chuckled in agreement and finished his glass as well. I glanced at the clock in the corner of the TV. Twenty minutes past midnight. The desire to return home and to real life was nonexistent. There, in that bar, was a dreamlike atmosphere, but reluctantly, I realized it was time to go.

"I don't want to, but I think we should leave. Tomorrow, we have class, then I have to work, you know..."

"Yes, I think you're right. At least one of us needs to be responsible."

He then asked for the bill, and I went to the bathroom. In the mirror, the image of a dizzy, red-cheeked Clara warmed my heart. I could see the contentment and pleasure written all over my face. I spent a few seconds contemplating the figure of my reflection, finding sincere beauty in every detail of me—even the ones I normally didn't find beautiful. Interesting, this thing of looking at yourself, leaving aside what is conventionally considered "beautiful." It didn't last long, so ingrained were these social ideas in my head, but it was a nice moment.

I went back to the bar; he had already paid the bill. I thanked him, and we left. Outside, the city was still awake, like any self-respecting metropolis. The cold night air slammed into my face, bringing me some sobriety. I started to walk to the subway, but John held me back with a gesture.

"I think it's better to take a cab. Kind of dangerous to ride the subway at this hour."

I agreed and we stood there waiting for a car to show up. After a few that already had passengers, we finally got a taxi. I felt, for a moment, as I still did constantly living in that country, like I was in a movie or a TV show. That classic scene: a date ending with someone getting into an iconic yellow car in New York City. Surrealisms of my life.

Contrary to what I expected, though, John got into the car with me.

"I just want to make sure you'll get home okay," he said after closing the door. I smiled in thanks and gave the taxi driver my address. I took the opportunity to observe the city from the window as we headed towards our destination. Most of the time, I got around on the subway, which made my eyes rarely meet those of the city. The night there was no different from the nights in São Paulo. Just like in my hometown, there were lights and cars and people. The ride didn't last long. When we arrived, I opened my bag to pay the driver, but John was faster and, once again, ended up paying the bill for me. I scolded him lightly but thanked him, at last.

We got out of the car, and he walked with me to the building's entrance.

"Thank you so much for accompanying me. You didn't have to do this."

"No problem, it was my pleasure."

I hesitated for a moment as I considered whether to invite him in. My body desperately craved more of that kiss, that touch, more of everything. On the other hand, it was a weekday, and a part of me, that hopelessly responsible part, decided it was best to let him go.

As I opened my lips to say goodbye, John surprised me with a kiss. So sudden, this one took my breath away in such a way that I felt all my strength leaving me. This time he was holding my neck, and his lips were so thirsty that it was impossible for me to reason. I hugged him by the shoulders, completely surrendered, not caring about possible vulnerabilities or judgments. With a soft moan into his mouth and my hands gripping his hair greedily, I made my desires clear. He responded to the voracity of the movements, his hands going from my neck to my hair and my face with great urgency—urgency that I could feel in his touch.

We interrupted the caresses for a moment. He took a deep breath as he looked at me in an indecipherable way. Meanwhile, I tried with all my might to regain the air which seemed to have been lost somewhere between my lips and my lungs. My heart was pounding uncontrollably, and my legs were shaking. John took my hands and kissed them hard, though his gesture had also something of a soft touch. Somehow, I managed to find the strength to speak, smiling at him. "Would you like to come inside?"

He closed his eyes for a brief second, expressing what seemed like an internal battle. He opened them again and, with a look that seemed to be at odds with himself, replied, "Believe me, I would love to! But tomorrow I have to wake up extremely early. I shouldn't even have gone out tonight, but I couldn't resist. I really wanted to see you."

I smiled understandingly, even though every part of my body ached in agonizing frustration.

"I understand. You're right, we better get some rest for tomorrow."

He tenderly kissed my forehead and then my hands again.

"Thank you for understanding."

"Of course! I had a great time today, thanks for the night!"

"I had a lot of fun too! See you tomorrow in class?"

"See you tomorrow."

I saw a taxi heading our way and signaled for it to stop.

"Good night, Clara." John kissed me on the lips once more. A very different kiss from the ones we had previously exchanged, just a touch of mouths without much depth. One of the many contrasts.

"Good night," I replied as I watched him get into the car.

I searched my purse for my keys, the sensations of the night still pulsing in me. With some difficulty, I entered the building. The short walk from the entrance to the elevator was an arduous one. My legs were wobbly, and my knees were taking some effort to move. Who would have thought that a first date could be so intense? Especially with someone I'd just met. From the introverted guy I'd barely noticed in the early days of class to the man who made my entire body crave more was a sudden, unpredictable transition.

I reached the apartment door and tried, without much success, to be as silent as possible. The keys jiggled more than I would have liked, the jingle echoing down the hall, loud, loud... when I finally unlocked the door, I found Kat fast asleep on the couch. I kicked off my shoes, tiptoed to my room. Arriving there, I threw my things on the floor and let myself fall on the bed and relive everything that had just happened. Again. And again. And again.

As I closed my eyes, I could feel John's touches. His scent was still fresh on my clothes and hair and I breathed in that scent deeply, permeating myself. I felt his strong lips, the taste of his saliva, the softness of his tongue entwined with mine. I relived the shivers running through my spine, my legs, my private parts... I forgot to experience the present.

I don't know at what point I fell asleep amid the frenzy I was in, but I remember waking up and realizing that I was still in the same clothes, lying on the bed in an uncomfortable position for my neck. I looked out the bedroom window; it was still dark out. I got up, went in search of my bag to find my cell phone, where I checked the time: three-thirty in the morning. Still in a semi-asleep state, I got up and put on my pajamas, put away my things that were lying on the floor, and lay down again.

I was more awake now, however, so I decided to keep fiddling with my phone until I fell asleep again. But, surprise! I came across an email from Dark Angel. I thought again about the night with John and concluded that having these two people in my life—an artistic spectrum in the virtual world and a palpable, voluptuous one in the real world—made me happy. I opened my online friend's message.

"Black Rose,

I've thought a lot about you today. It's funny how someone I don't know can touch me so intensely. All the art that we usually ignore in our daily lives (logos on mugs, pictures on birthday cards, designs for work websites...) became so evident to me after we started talking.

I hope you don't think I'm crazy for sharing these thoughts with you. I'm a very ordinary and boring person actually. And, to be quite honest, I'm not tech-savvy for anything that doesn't have to do with work. Anyway, I'm saying all this so you don't think I'm a creepy freak who spends all day living a virtual life. I just want us to continue our cyber friendship.

And please don't stop posting your drawings.

Dark Angel"

As if the overwhelming emotions of that night were not enough, still very fresh in my memory, now I was also experiencing the euphoria of having my ego graced by that stranger who was already part of my life. Explosions inside me. Never before had I thought I would have any impact on anyone else, let alone regarding art. Let alone for having posted unpretentious scribbles on the internet. I responded promptly.

"Dark Angel,

I was very happy to read your email! I never intended to reach anyone by exposing my drawings online. In fact, I'm not sure why I decided to do it, but it was worth it just because I got to 'meet' you. Even though I produce art sometimes, I myself miss all these things you mentioned. I think we are made up not to pay attention to what is not part of practical life.

As for thinking you're crazy, I've never thought that, not for a moment. Maybe I should, and maybe the fact that I didn't suspect you makes me the crazy one. But I just go along with my instincts, and they tell me that you, like me, are just an 'ordinary' human being, whatever that means.

Xoxo,

Black Rose"

After hitting the send button, I put my phone down, closed my eyes. I thought it would take a while for me to fall back to sleep, but somnolence soon sheltered me in its welcoming arms. For the rest of the night, I was filled with colorful and absurd dreams, which would disappear from my memory as soon as I woke up to consciousness. The core of the illogical, however, would wander in my head, as it should.

My waking up was peaceful, despite the few hours of sleep, the drunkenness, and the ecstasy of the night before. I felt energized as if something inside me had awakened after a long time of hibernation, numbness. And I followed my morning rituals of all the other days as if that one, in particular, wasn't welcoming the change from within. I took a shower, chose my clothes for college (this time, I confess with some embarrassment, a little more carefully than the rest of the days), had breakfast, etc., etc., etc.

The walk to the subway was a little more leisurely that day. I tried to observe what art there was in my way, inspired by the experiences of Dark Angel. Unlike in São Paulo, graffiti was not everywhere. Some specific spots, like Brooklyn, had art on the walls, but the practice was not as much a part of the New York culture as it was in my hometown. However, when your eyes search for that specific something, finding it becomes relatively easy. For example, a blackboard sign in front of a café. The daily specials were written in white chalk, as well as the more classic orders and their prices. Above all, the word *"Café,"* in green chalk and a calligraphic font, stood out, and, next to the small menu, a drawing of a brown cup. There was no exceptional artistic skill there, but there was certain affection, one could see. And that sight of the simple sign in some coffee shop made me smile.

In addition to that discovery, I saw other small remnants of art: stickers on windows, shop signs, patterns on the clothes of people who passed by me... how much beauty there was in the trivialities of everyday life! I continued to observe, finding delight and beauty, proportions, symmetries, harmonies... all the way to the university. It wasn't until I got there that I remembered that I'd meet John in class. The thought made me a little apprehensive.

Before entering the building where today's class was to be held, I sat on a bench for a moment, pondering, reflecting. John was a shy and withdrawn guy, and he barely spoke to anyone. The night before, we'd almost slept together, and today, having healed from the effects of the many beers he'd had, he was perhaps more aware that he'd exchanged kisses and caresses with a person he would have to see almost every day for the next two years. Not that I expected anything from him in particular—or did I? But men, they have this tendency to think that women's expectations are always too much for them. And a habit of thinking they know what we want, of course. Even more so the Americans, with their withdrawal shades, false puritans. I didn't want him to be uncomfortable or to feel like he needed to act in any specific way with me. But in the end, I concluded the obvious, that I could do nothing to control the thoughts or feelings of others. Sigh.

I was about to get up to head to the classroom when I felt someone approaching. It was John, of course. He looked even more handsome than usual that day, perhaps because I was on a journey to observe the beauty in life, perhaps because my vision of him now involved the captivation that comes from feelings. He wore his usual black leather jacket and carried two large cups of coffee in his hands. I couldn't hold back a smile when I saw him, which he timidly returned. When he reached me, he offered me one of the cups and sat on the bench by my side.

"Thanks," I told him, picking up the coffee cup and taking a sip.

"Black with sweetener, right?" he said as he sipped his own.

I smiled once more as I replied, "That's right. You remembered."

We didn't say anything for the next few seconds, taking the opportunity to enjoy the drinks and the silence, which, contrary to what I thought, wasn't uncomfortable at all. It was, in fact, the opposite. That stillness had something of a welcoming aura, as if words were no longer a necessary crutch in each other's presence. Coziness. At one point, however, he broke the silence. "How did you sleep?"

"Well," I said, "I haven't had many hours of sleep, but I don't feel tired. And you?"

"To tell you the truth, I must have only slept a couple of hours. I had to wake up very early to do some work, and that made me anxious, which made me not able to sleep much. Besides," he hesitated for a moment, lowering his gaze before continuing, "I thought about you all night, which also kept me awake."

Once again, as if my face had a life of its own, I couldn't help but smile at his words. He seemed to be anxiously waiting for my answer. Finally, I told him, "I thought about you all night, too."

For a moment, I felt like I was lying, as my night had been an explosion of emotions that not only had to do with him, but Dark Angel as well. But the feeling soon passed, listening to my rational side. After all, how could I even compare the intangible virtual friend with the man whose scent had lingered in my body for all those night hours?

He smiled at my answer and, to my surprise, got closer to my face and pressed his lips against mine in a tender kiss. The sensations of the night before returned instantly, even in the face of such a soft and sweet touch. My heartbeat became loud, resonant, in a rhythm that reminded me of the most striking notes of classic music—a fierce, raw harmony; but as beautiful as unreachable flames. Continuous shivers down my back and legs, the fire, burning... in the few seconds that the kiss lasted.

We turned our attention to the coffees once more, casually, as if I wasn't completely enraptured. I noticed a small movement around us, realizing it was the other students who were heading to their respective classes. Suddenly, life returned to normal, and the world had more inhabitants than just the two of us. What a pity.

"I think we better go inside," I said to John, who nodded as he got to his feet.

We went on, then, without saying anything else until we reached the classroom. There, almost every seat was already taken. We sat in a corner, not too far apart, but not close enough to be able to talk.

Then I saw Elena, who was also a little distant, at a desk in front of me. She looked in my direction and smiled warmly at me. I returned her gesture, and when she realized I had turned my attention to her, she winked mischievously. I laughed internally. She knew things, Elena. She had probably noticed that I had arrived there with John. She drew her conclusions, of course.

The teacher did not take long to arrive, and we all turned our attention to him. The class was somewhat interesting, but that didn't make me fully concentrate on his words. In my head, all the recent events, from the intense encounter with John to the messages from Dark Angel to the innocent kiss received a few minutes ago, circulated with intensity in a background of thoughts. I wanted—no, needed—somehow to put all those emotions to some use. Otherwise, I would end up flirting with madness; I already was, actually. I opened a notebook, then, and began sketching with a pencil. I didn't know what would come out of it, but the urge to express myself was quickly taking shape on that paper, flowing, flowing...

My scribbles, in the end, represented a random woman lying on the sand of a random beach, naked, with a soft smile. The sea, in the background, showed its indomitable side, with angry waves that broke when they reached the shore. On either side of the woman, in the distance, two silhouettes of men could be seen walking towards her. I looked at that sketch and felt like making a painting out of it. Colors were missing, something beyond the shading that the tools I had on hand allowed me. So I decided: after work, I would look for an art supply store. That decision touched my heart—so much so that I could barely contain myself. Internal explosion—implosion.

For the rest of the classes, tranquility. After drawing, expressing, satisfying, I managed to concentrate and the thoughts that, from time to time, came to my mind were no longer accompanied by violent sensations of lack of control. At times, barely perceptible specks of time, John would turn in my direction—quick smiles. Other than that, he was just as usual, quiet, his face buried in books for most of the time.

At the end of the day, he approached me while I packed my things to leave.

"Hey, Clara," he said, and my name sounded like something magical as it left his lips. He had said it in his usual accent, but this time slowly and softly, almost like a song.

"Hey," I replied, stopping what I was doing and turning to him.

"I'm super busy with work today and for the rest of the week, actually. But I wanted to know if you want to do something this weekend."

His manner of speaking contained, as always, a certain apprehension. It was sweet the way he didn't know, but the fact that he was trying said something about his interest in me—I felt certain power. Once again, I smiled at him in a way that would ease his worries. And replied, "Sure, I would love to. I work this Saturday, but I leave at seven."

His expression showed relief and then a sudden unease.

"I need to run now, but will I see you the day after tomorrow?"

"Yes, see you in class then."

Before hurriedly leaving, he kissed me on the cheek softly, leaving a silly smile on my face. I barely noticed Elena approaching as soon as he left.

"What's going on with you two?" the blonde asked, sitting down on a chair next to me and pulling it close.

"Well... we went out last night."

She made an exaggerated expression of surprise, opening her eyes as widely as she could and placing her hands on her cheeks as if I'd just told her a federal secret. Elena was always a lot.

"Tell me everything."

I then tried, in a direct and neutral manner, to detail the event. She was smiling broadly as she listened to my narration, and I felt like a teenager again, sharing stories of the boy I liked with a high school friend. When it was over, she looked ecstatic.

"And are you going out again this week?"

"Apparently, yes."

She clapped her hands enthusiastically, and I couldn't help but chuckle with delight.

"You need to let me live through you, so be sure to tell me all the details!"

"What do you mean 'live through me'?" I answered her between laughs.

"Well, I'm married. I love my life and my husband, but I will never have a first date again. Or a first kiss, first time in bed..."

"Don't worry, I'll tell you everything."

She smiled in thanks and then said goodbye. I needed to go, too, as my shift would soon begin. I started walking to the subway and, just like when coming to college that morning, continued to observe the art around me. I wondered how I ever managed not to see all that, so evidently the beauty now jumped out at me. It was amazing how, in a world as chaotic as ours, people didn't forget that the subtleties of emotions expressed by art also mattered.

⟫⟫⟫ ⟪⟪⟪

I nside the subway, sitting on one of the crowded seats, I took my cell phone out of my pocket and checked my email. Dark Angel had answered me—my contentment, already present, screaming, almost aching, rose once more, reaching levels I never thought possible in a surf of waves that almost drown me, just almost. Here's what his message said.

"Black Rose,
Wow, you wrote to me in the middle of the night! Insomnia? It doesn't matter, I'm glad you took the time to send me this message.
I'm also glad you don't distrust me. I don't have any uncertainty about you either, but, of course, I have the privilege of having known you through your art, which makes this process a lot easier.
In fact, I think the world we live in is made in such a way that we don't appreciate these little great gems of life. That is a shame. But I believe we can still change that, starting with ourselves. That's

why I set out to observe art wherever I am, at least once a day.

Thank you once again for awakening these insights in me. I hope what keeps you up at night is a good thing, and if not, I wish you are able to transform it with your admirable gift.

Xoxo,
Dark Angel"

I finished reading the email, and there was this caress in my heart as if calming the gale of so many things inside. I decided to answer him right away and started typing, although awkwardly, holding my bag in my lap, and surrounded by people. Those New York subway seats were positioned against the walls of the train, and at rush hour, everyone leaned and jostled with people to their right and left and in front. But that was okay.

"Dark Angel,
Thanks for the concern, but I did not have insomnia. I got home late last night. That's why I was up.

Speaking of art, I made a sketch today that I intend to turn into a painting. I'm really excited to get back to painting! I will post a picture when it's finished.

I also wanted to thank you for telling me about your observations and how you discovered 'hidden' art in everyday things. I started doing the same, trying to see the art around me, and it completely changed my day.

I'm happy to rediscover the artistic spark inside me and also to have someone to share what I do with. Thanks again for appreciating my work.

Xoxo,

Black Rose"

After sending it, I realized again how excited I was to start turning that draft of mine into a painting. There was an arts and crafts store near work, and I planned to stop by after my shift. The next day, I wouldn't have class, and I decided to start painting then. Sadly, I couldn't remember the last time I'd done it. Probably when I was still in middle school for some project in Art class. The thought haunted me a little, how easy it was to put aside passions that should be the pulse.

My train arrived at the station, and I headed to the diner. There weren't many customers that day, so I spent most of my time cleaning. I liked it better when I didn't have to deal with people at work. I took advantage of the time spent on the monotonous task to delve into the fantasies that had been so present in my thoughts lately. In my daydreams, I separated very clearly, as always, John from Dark Angel. It was funny how my mind couldn't conceive of a world where they coexisted. It made me reflect. I noticed, for example, that I hadn't mentioned to John that I liked to draw and paint. We never even talked about art, actually. It was as if I were two people at the same time, and they were so different that they lived in distinct universes. But the two actually inhabited me. Paradoxes, in conclusion.

My head wandered between reflections and fantasies as I cleaned the coffee pot when my boss called me—I woke up to reality then. I put the cleaning utensils aside and walked over to him. He asked me to accompany him to his office. I wondered what he would have to talk to me about in there. If he needed to call me out on something, he didn't hesitate to do it in front of everyone.

We got inside, and I closed the door behind me. He pointed to the chair in front of his desk. "Please, sit down."

I sat down awkwardly as he took a seat and glanced at some papers that were strewn across the table.

"Clara, you're a great employee," he began, and like every time he spoke, I had to work hard to understand his words because of the thick accent.

I nodded in thanks for the statement. I waited for him to continue.

"But you work here without papers." He paused for a long time as if to make sure I understood him. I knew what he was talking about, of course. My visa in that country was a student one and, technically, I was prohibited from working while I was in school. So all the jobs I'd had, including waitressing, were informal. Again, I nodded to assure him I understood.

"I can't have employees without papers anymore. I'm getting my American citizenship. It's very dangerous not to comply with the law."

I was a little shocked for a few seconds. In disbelief, I asked, "Are you firing me?"

He nodded regretfully.

"I'm sorry, Clara. You can finish your shift and then take your paycheck."

I stayed there. Still. Not knowing what to do next. It was the first time in my life that I had been fired. I felt something weird in my chest, a nameless thing. No, no, it did have a name: rejection. After a few seconds half-paralyzed, my boss coughed in a way that suggested the subject was closed—which made me get up and leave the room at last. I went back to the task of cleaning the coffee machine, still a little in disbelief, thinking, thinking... what would come next? I would need to look for another job. I had saved money for a long time in Brazil before coming to the United States, but my savings were basically to pay for school costs. I needed to work to pay the rent, bills, food...

The rest of the day passed as if in slow-motion, populated with thoughts of "why." I got fired, and yet I smiled more than ever at customers. I cleaned the tables with surgical care. I took out the trash, even though it was not my turn to do it. And at some point I didn't see coming, my shift ended. I went to my boss to give back my uniform and collect my money for the week. It wasn't much. It was still Wednesday, and I would only receive payment for the first part of the week. I hadn't quite gotten used to being paid weekly, so my finances were a little bit of a chaos. But despite that, I thanked myself for having the habit of always saving a little money, which would hold up for a little while. I said goodbye to him and to my coworkers quickly. They wished me good luck, see you later, etc., robotic—no big fuss. Life would go on as usual for them: serving customers, complaining, cleaning, getting paid, returning home and then back to work... just without the Brazilian girl, the only one without a Hispanic accent who made everyone have to speak English instead of Spanish, the native language of all the other employees.

I left the diner still feeling weird, different. I was worried, but at the same time, if I was honest with myself, a little relieved. This whole dealing with people thing was exhausting. People are tough animals. Also, the job was very physically demanding as well. I was always running around with orders or cleaning up, and at the end of the day, my body was always exhausted. Thinking about it, still a little emotional, I quickly took stock of things and decided to go back to babysitting. The money wasn't so good, but I liked dealing with children better than with adults. There's the feeling of being such a crucial part of the formation of a little person and all the teachings and love they give without caring about the things that grown-ups do.

I walked towards home, my plans to buy the painting supplies fading as my source of income had just dwindled. But, alas! with nothing to look forward to occupying my time, it was worth "losing" a few dollars to help myself face the many and such strong feelings that have been plaguing me lately. I wondered if the amplitude of such sensations had anything to do with the fact that I was in a different country, no family, no friends... and I concluded that it made a lot of sense. It was not easy to deal with life alone, and the weight of being an adult, increasingly palpable, was evident in me.

I arrived at the store, at last, my heart already singing at the thought that I would be painting again soon. I started looking for the necessary supplies and filling my shopping basket. That place was an Eden for arts and crafts lovers. Everything from wood art to confectionery materials inhabited the almost magical shelves—a world of possibilities, art to be created, just waiting to be born. I had to control myself to stick to the basics. I bought three medium-sized canvases, assorted brushes, different colored paints, and an apron.

When I got home, I went straight to my room, moved the things that occupied my study desk, and put my painting materials on it. I changed into an old T-shirt and shorts, put my apron over everything, picked up the sketch I'd made in class, finally sat down to start working. I began the process by reproducing the drawing on my blank canvas, adding more details as I did so. After I was satisfied, I put the black pencil aside and opened my paints, the colors ready to be part of the work. I let my instincts lead my brush to the shades that would be part of the painting without thinking too much about the combinations that were born with each brushstroke. It was certainly very difficult not to rationalize every step I took in life, even for small things, but at that moment, I didn't have to make an effort to do so. I think I was being taken over by forces beyond my comprehension. I didn't worry about what the final product would look like; I just dedicated myself to enjoying the process.

I'm not sure how much time had passed while I was painting, but I finally reached the journey's end. I was feeling a pleasant tiredness, a serene satisfaction, like at the end of a yoga session. Or right after an orgasm. Or a massage. I finally looked at my painting. The sea at the bottom had a clear blue mixed with greenish tones, and I could see the violent movements of the waves, which died when they reached the white sand. The woman lying on the beach had long, black hair that covered her bare breasts, and her genitals were hidden by the position of her legs, one extended and the other half-bent. The men coming at her from opposite directions were just distant black silhouettes.

I contemplated my work for a long time. An unspeakable pride. It was a beautiful painting, and I had given everything I had to make it take shape. My soul smiled with joy and satisfaction, and I loved myself at that moment, perhaps more than any other, for being able to produce something that had given me so much pleasure and that I could admire indefinitely. I signed my painting "CS," for Clara da Silva. It wasn't Black Rose's work, though she would be the one who would send it to my Dark Angel—it was mine, Clara's. I also wanted to create a name for the painting. I was always very frustrated when the paintings I liked didn't have a title. I don't know why. So I decided to call it "The Worlds of a Woman."

After cleaning up the mess, I left the painting to dry on the desk and went to take a shower. There were ink stains on my hands and arms and even a splash of blue color on my face. As I came out of the bathroom, a towel wrapped around my head and another around my body, I ran into Kat, who had just gotten home from work.

"Hi, girl." I greeted her casually and she smiled and replied as she set her purse down on the couch.

"Hi, Clara. How was your day?"

"Well, I... got fired."

She looked at me with a mixture of surprise, concern, and empathy.

"Damn, I can't believe it! I'm sorry! Are you okay?"

I smiled at her calmly as I replied. "Yes, I am. It's not like I loved that job, anyway. And I know I can get another one soon. Oh, and don't worry about the rent and the bills, I have a reserve."

"No, you don't worry about it, please! You can rest easy and take the time you need to get another job. I can take care of things in the meantime."

I was moved by her reaction. Maybe we were better friends than I thought and I just hadn't realized it yet. With each passing day, I learned that Americans showed their feelings in a completely different way from Brazilians, and these cultural nuances gradually became part of me.

"Thank you, Kat, really."

As I looked for pajamas to put on that night, full of simple plans—watching a movie, sipping on an indulgent glass of wine maybe—I heard the familiar notification sound coming from my cell phone. I looked at the screen: new email from Dark Angel. I smiled excitedly; I couldn't wait to show him my painting. I then opened the message from my virtual friend.

"Black Rose,
It fills my heart with joy knowing that you've decided to paint, and how happy it seems to make

you. I can't wait to see your creation! I'm sure it will be as amazing as everything else I've seen of your art so far.

I'm glad it wasn't insomnia that plagued you that night, as it's a preferable companion not to have. I've suffered from this curse for most of my life, and I wouldn't wish it on my worst enemy.

This thing of looking at the art around us is really funny. Once you start, you can't ignore it. Today, for example, I was barely able to concentrate in a meeting, so caught up I was in the geometric shapes of a coworker's ultra-colored tie. The thing was so blatant to me that it was impossible to take my attention away from it, although no one else seemed to notice.

Anyway, I need to get my feet on the ground and get back to reality, at least when I'm working. But I feel very privileged to have all this happening inside my head, opening myself up to new emotions and sensations that only art can provide. I even decided to visit an art gallery this weekend. I've never been to one of these places before, but why not, right? I'll tell you all about my adventure after.

I hope your day has been good. Be sure to post your painting as soon as it's ready, ok?

Xoxo,
Dark Angel"

I finished reading the email and caught myself in an idea—fanciful, perhaps, but nothing less than real. I realized how much I had influenced that life, who began to observe art to the point where he became interested in visiting a gallery. It was a strange feeling, as if he, like my painting, was also a "creation" of mine. And for a strange, dangerous moment, I wanted him to be more than an online alias. I wanted to accompany him to the gallery, admire the paintings, talk about how artists give us so many clues of what they want to express with their work—by the way they brush, by the colors chosen, by the details and materials and shadings and tones... I imagined myself walking among the canvases with this faceless man, drinking red wine, trying to unlock the secrets of art.

The thought fell apart. What would I gain from ruining the magic of what Dark Angel meant to me? If he suddenly had a name, a face, and a story, he would no longer be the mystery that gave our relationship meaning—so platonic, yet so real. I pushed the fantasies out of my head and decided to respond to his email.

"*Dark Angel,*

Have a great time in the gallery! I'm sure it will be an amazing experience for you, given your artistic sensibility. Tell me all about it, and let me know if you decide to buy any paintings. I'd love to know what attributes a painting has to have to catch your eye enough for you to want to take it home.

Yeah, this thing of observing art in everyday life can be dangerous, especially when you have to pay attention to work. I also get very distracted by this (and by my endless daydreaming). I hope that your coworkers start to wear more sober ties, as I believe that would help a lot. In any case, you should also wear some exaggeratedly colored accessories to get back at them.

I also had insomnia once. It's not cool at all, and I imagine that going through it for so long is even worse. I hope you don't suffer from this anymore. When I did, the lack of sleep affected my whole life. I was always in a bad mood, couldn't concentrate on anything, and my body was always tired.

Regarding my painting, I finished it today. I'm waiting for the paint to dry so I can put it up on the wall, and then I'll take a picture to post on the blog. Although, you being the only person accessing my page, I think it would be easier to send you the photo via email. I'll think about it.

I hope your day has been good. Mine has had its
ups and downs, but I'm glad I completed my work.
 Xoxo,
Black Rose"

After sending the message, I stayed on my phone, navigating the waters of social media. I came across some photos of friends in Brazil having fun at a barbecue. I was moved with *saudade*, that word that is so ours, with no translation. *Saudade*: nostalgia, or homesickness, I guess. I thought of the pre-Internet era, when people were forced to communicate by letter. There were no faces, no voices, and if something happened, you couldn't find out right away. I lived through that era as a teenager, but I couldn't figure out how I did things. No GPS, no internet on my phone, no camera... no knowledge. Suddenly, there were no more walls between online life and offline life. Deliberating on it, scrolling down all my timelines, liking, liking... Dark Angel replied to my email. I went to my inbox.

"Black Rose,
 My day was good, but only because I made it that
way. You know, work can sometimes (most of the
time) be quite stressful.

I'm so glad you finished your painting! I can't wait to see it, and in my humble opinion, while I'm flattered by the prospect of receiving a photo of your work via email, I think you should post it on your blog. You never know, right? If I 'fell' onto your page by accident, others might, too, and I would hate to deprive them of admiring your art.

Yeah, about insomnia, I know what you mean about it affecting your whole life. I was so tired at the time that I couldn't concentrate on the smallest day-to-day tasks, like doing my homework when I was still a schoolboy or reading a book or a newspaper. But today, fortunately, I am no longer afflicted with this harmful disease (if I can call it that).

I love the extravagant tie idea. I think I'll put that into practice tomorrow at the office. Surely it will draw my coworkers' attention to me (and possibly get me sent to HR to do a psychological profile or something) since I'm always pretty sober regarding my work clothes. I will have a good laugh at the reactions of the people around me.

I hadn't considered the possibility of acquiring a painting from the gallery, but now I'm excited at the prospect. It would be the first time I buy art. I feel like a refined adult now. I should start hosting some cheese and wine tasting dinners with classical music in the background to match the newfound sophistication (I hope you can detect the sarcasm here).

Anyway, have a great day tomorrow!
Xoxo,
Dark Angel"

I laughed as I read his email, at his sarcastic sense of humor, a bit like mine. I realized that, little by little, the layers of his personality were making themselves present in our conversations and, probably, mine as well. It was really nice to have someone to talk to, even if I couldn't fully open up to him. I was going to respond to his email, but I got interrupted by Kat, who knocked on my bedroom door and asked if she could come in.

"Of course, the door is open."

My roommate came inside and asked me to zip up her dress. She looked stunning. Her blond hair had been curled with a curling iron, and light make-up enhanced her prettiest features. Her big blue eyes were glowing. The tight red dress accentuated her hips, and the black boots with gigantic heels, completed the alluring aura. After helping her with the zipper, she turned to me, placing her hands on her hips, and asked, "So, what do you think? Too much? I think so, right? Should I wear the blue dress instead? Or do I change the shoes?"

I could see that Kat was nervous, something new to me. I had never seen her like this, especially before a date. I tried to convey some calm with my eyes, smiled, and replied, "You look beautiful. You don't need to change a thing, in my opinion."

She smiled back and nodded in gratitude. Then her expression returned to one of apprehension.

"What's going on?" I asked. "Why are you so nervous? It's been so long since you and Jordan have been dating."

She then sat on the edge of my bed and, after taking a deep breath, explained. "I think he's going to propose."

I was in shock for a few seconds, thinking about their relationship. They were already together when I moved into the apartment, and, according to my roommate, they had started dating almost a year before that. However, they did not define themselves as a real couple; I even witnessed Kat going on dates with other guys. The fact that she thought he was going to ask her to marry him was something I couldn't fathom.

"How so? Why do you think that?"

"Well, these last few weeks he's been especially romantic, wanting to see me all the time and talking about how important I am in his life. And then he asked me on this date tonight at this super fancy restaurant and said he had news. He said it was serious."

It took me a few more seconds to process. I had seen him a few times, although we never really talked. But from what I'd seen, and from what Kat told me, Jordan seemed to be the definition of an immature man, one who would never commit to someone so seriously. "Boys will be boys," as the American saying goes. "Men are like that," etc., etc. They hadn't even made the relationship official, and he himself agreed that he didn't want to be committed to a person in that way. And Kat was completely in agreement with that.

"Isn't he just going to talk about your relationship becoming official?" I suggested.

"No, we talked about it a few days ago. I joked about putting a label on our relationship and his response was: 'If we were going to do that, I would definitely put a ring on your finger instead of just changing the status to "dating" on social media.'"

"Wow... and what are you going to say if he proposes?"

She hesitated for a few seconds, ran her hand nervously through a lock of her hair.

"I...well, I'll have to say no. I can't marry Jordan, this is crazy! I'm far too young anyway, and if I were to marry someone now, it wouldn't be him. I mean, not that I don't like him that way, but... can you imagine him as a husband?"

I shook my head "no."

"Exactly! This is all so crazy! And the worst part is that, after tonight, we're going to have to stop hanging out. You can't go back to normal after saying no to a marriage proposal. And I didn't want to break up with him. I... you know, I like him."

Without thinking too much, I hugged her. There was nothing to say—only an attempt to comfort her seemed to fit there. She didn't react at first, and I believe she was surprised by my gesture. But then she returned the hug, and we stayed like that for a good while. Then I moved back and said, "I'm sorry you're going through this, but...maybe it's a good thing that you guys break up. Maybe that way you can focus on you and, who knows, after a while, be able to fully give yourself to a relationship. I don't think that will happen as long as you have Jordan around."

She smiled with her lips, though her eyes were still sad.

"Yeah, you're probably right. Well, I'm gonna go. When I get back, if you're awake, I'll let you know how it went."

I nodded, and Kat disappeared through the door, closing it behind her. I thought about what she was experiencing—I would definitely rather be single, yes. I repeated this to myself over and over again. I wondered, though, if that status would stay the same for long, given that I was dating John now. I visualized him: his features, his touch, our conversations. I was already feeling something like... missing him?... even though I had seen him the day before. Also, I couldn't wait to see him the next morning in class.

My thoughts then turned once more to Kat. Her birthday was coming up. I hoped this thing with Jordan wouldn't ruin her day. I still had no idea what to get her. Buying for someone you don't know doesn't leave much room for creativity. Whatever. A purse, a perfume... something neutral to exempt myself but, at the same time, show that I care. It couldn't be expensive either—but come to think of it, I was in the land of consumerism, and a lot of things were ridiculously cheap.

My mind was an infinite number of thoughts at times. It flew here and there and here again.

I thought then that I needed, as soon as possible, to start looking for a new job. As soon as I arrived in the United States, I had signed up for a website that offered babysitting and nannying services to families, where I got my first job in that country.

Then a friend of Kat's referred me to the waitress one I'd just lost.

I turned on my computer and accessed that site, reactivating my registration. I spent a few minutes looking through the job openings. Nothing is more depressing than facing the baseness of capitalism, but I applied for some jobs; there was no remedy. Then I decided to relax a little. I felt a sense of worthiness in comforting myself. It had been a long day.

I turned off the computer, then went to the table where my painting rested and admired my work once more. It wasn't completely dry yet—but the thrilling anticipation told me I could already hang it up. There were no nails there, but a kind of hook that you could "stick" to the wall without ruining it. My room was full of them, some occupied with pictures of my life in Brazil, others holding scarves and hats, and others empty. I chose one right above my bed and hung my painting there. I liked the way it complemented the rest of the décor. It had something harmonious without being symmetrical, I don't know. With my cell phone camera, I took some pictures. I decided to post it on my blog. You never know. That's what Dark Angel told me. I still hadn't replied to his last email. I lay on my bed, went back to my inbox to write to him.

"Dark Angel,

Indeed, work can be quite stressful. Some jobs more than others, of course. Although I don't have to worry about that for now—I got fired today. But that's okay, it wasn't my dream job or anything.

I decided to publish the photo of my painting on the blog. In fact, I intend to do so as soon as I finish writing this email. Thanks for encouraging me to do this. You know, you say I've inspired you to look at the art around you and all, but you've inspired me to keep creating. The same thing happens to me every time: I have a colossal flow of inspiration and I produce and produce until, all of a sudden, I stop and do nothing productive again for years on end. But not this time.

I'm glad insomnia is no longer in your life. There are so many of these diseases (I think, yes, we can call them that) that affect the modern world that it is difficult not to find yourself a victim of at least one of them. How did you manage to beat the lack of sleep? I had to resort to meds for a while, but then I didn't need them anymore. It's pretty crazy, by the way, how a small pill of three grams is able to give a solution to problems that, many times, have their origin in external events, experiences, feelings...

I think it would be great for you, who dress so seriously, to add a little color to your everyday life, even if it makes people around you see you as a nutcase. It may even be that you inspire someone. Who knows what's in the lives of each of your coworkers, you know? Maybe you'll start a revolution in the office.

I loved the idea of the cheese and wine tasting. This definitely gets you one step closer to getting the refined adult card. Of course, they only give us the official one after playing a lot of golf, buying a boat, and putting up a white picket fence around the house, but you are already taking a step on that path.

Hope your day is amazing tomorrow too!

Xoxo,

Black Rose"

After sending the email, I went to my blog page. I spent a long time trying to select the best photo to publish as if that poorly visited virtual space was of paramount importance—what for?—; I finally chose one where the light seemed better to me. The caption: "The Worlds of a Woman — oil on canvas."

I don't know when I fell asleep, but I woke up with my cell phone beside me, the black screen reflecting my sleepy and still confused eyes with the memory lapse that happens in waking up. As a first instinct of every morning, I reached for it, only to find out I was late for school. I got up at once, put on the first clothes I saw, brushed my teeth, grabbed my bag, ran out the door. A rush of adrenaline in the usually peaceful routine.

I hurried to the subway. On my seat, I was finally able to breathe a little. I looked at my phone again, the old habit, and saw that Dark Angel had answered me, but I decided to read his email after class when things were calmer. The truth is, I didn't want to have such a fresh memory of him at that moment, as I would soon see John.

The subway that day was slower than usual, and when I finally arrived at the university, the first class had already started. When I discreetly opened the door, the professor was pointing to his slides as he spoke and didn't see me enter. I looked around quickly and saw John from behind, his leather jacket slung over the back of his chair, as usual. Lucky for me, there was an empty seat next to him, and I sat there. He turned to me and smiled. I returned his smile. He muttered, almost inaudibly, "You're late."

And as he spoke, he placed a cup of coffee on my desk. I hadn't noticed he had two. I whispered, "I overslept. Thank you so much for the coffee! I didn't have time to eat anything before leaving."

I sipped it, enjoying the indescribable satisfaction. All I needed in the morning was caffeine. I don't even know if the thing really gave me energy or if it was just another habit that we believe does something inside us—it doesn't really matter.

After the class ended, I was still jotting some things down on my notebook when I felt John's hand gently grip my arm. I turned to him. I smiled. It was easy to smile. He said, "I can't wait for the weekend!"

I put my pen aside and replied, "Me neither."

"I was going to tell you that I'm basically free for the entire weekend. We can go out on Saturday night and, on Sunday, maybe have lunch together. If you're available, of course."

"Sounds good to me. And as for being available, recently my schedule has been extremely empty."

He looked puzzled.

"What do you mean?"

"Well, I... got fired yesterday."

John took both my hands and looked me straight in the eyes with sorrow.

"I'm sorry, Clara. Are you okay?"

"Yes, I am. It was a waitressing job; it's not like it was my dream job. And I'm already looking for other things, anyway."

"Well, if you need anything, just let me know, okay?"

"Thank you, John."

After that, we just stood there, hands still joined and eyes still connected, for a long time. Those things I felt every time I was in his presence came back in full force. I was also touched by his willingness to help me. With what, I don't know; it didn't matter. I couldn't tell if what I was feeling was merely physical or something else. All I know is that I had to make a huge effort to control the urge to throw myself at him aggressively, kiss him, grab him right there in the classroom, not let him walk away from me ever again.

"I need to go to the bathroom before the next class." John broke the silence, waking me up to reality.

"Oh, yes, I... I do too."

We left the room and went our separate ways. The men's restrooms were one floor above ours while the women's restrooms were in that same hallway. I got there, washed my face, took a deep breath. Every time I interacted with John, it was the same thing. I hadn't known anyone in a while who made me feel so frantically voluptuous. Once again, I splashed some water on my face, and while I was drying it, a girl came into the bathroom. I had seen her in the halls a few times. She looked anxious to see me. I nodded, smiling warmly, and she smiled back.

I returned my attention to my reflection in the mirror. My cheeks were rosy, and my eyes were anxious. I opened the bag I had taken with me to see if there was any makeup there with the naive intention of disguising my very evident lust, but I found only a powder foundation that was practically gone. I vigorously rubbed the sponge that came with the package into the product, but it only picked up a few remnants of the powder. I applied it to my face anyway. It didn't make much of a difference.

"Do you want mine?"

I turned to the side and noticed that the girl was watching me and had offered me her makeup bag. She continued, "Our skin has a similar tone. I have a liquid foundation, compact powder, and concealer, whatever you want to use."

I took the toiletry bag from her hand and smiled in relief, a feeling of having been saved.

"Thank you so much! I ran out of the house today and didn't have time to put on makeup or anything, and there's this guy in my class... Well, he makes me a little... uneasy... and I just wanted to make sure he wouldn't notice that my face is so flushed."

"I completely understand."

"Oh, my name is Clara." I held out my hand, which she shook firmly.

"Nice to meet you. I am... My name is Alex."

"Nice to meet you too."

I took a look at the products she had and decided to apply some foundation and set it with the powder, just to take the redness off my face. While I was doing this, she was touching up her nude lipstick.

"I'm in Creative Writing classes," Alex started to say casually. "And you?"

"I'm in Human Resources."

"Cool."

"Not really, actually. But Creative Writing... it must be amazing!"

"Yeah, I like it a lot. I've been writing since I was little. Not that it's a very profitable career idea, but I didn't want to spend so much time and money on something that didn't make me happy, you know?"

"I understand." I understood, of course. "It takes courage to think like that in a world like ours. A courage that I don't have."

"You don't like your courses?"

"Yes, I do. But I don't love it."

She nodded and proceeded to fix her hair. In the mirror, we saw that a woman was entering the bathroom. She was still holding the door with one hand when she glanced our way and turned back, closing the door behind her. I frowned in puzzlement and looked at Alex questioningly, who didn't seem surprised.

"Um... what was that all about?" I asked, mostly to myself. However, she answered my question.

"She didn't want to share a bathroom with me."

By that time, I was done with the makeup and gave her the toiletry bag back. Still confused, I asked, "Why not?"

Alex smiled an odd smile, a mixture of sadness and irony in her expression.

"I'm a trans woman."

"Ah. I'm sorry people treat you that way. I wish humanity was more...humane."

She smiled, authentically this time, and replied, "It was nothing. These things happen, I barely notice it anymore after so long."

"Thanks again for the makeup, you saved my day. I have to go. The next class is about to start."

"Yeah, me too. See you around?"

"Yes, see you."

I walked back to the classroom, thinking about the look on the face of the girl who didn't want to go into the same bathroom Alex was in—revulsion, nausea. My brain didn't quite compute such a reaction, although this was, beyond common, actually expected. And it pained me to think that that was nothing compared to the many other things she had to go through in her life—a lump in my throat, discomfort, and guilt for bringing that pain to me, on top of my privilege. And all just for being. But certain existences were, if not invisible, intolerable.

⋙ ⋘

The rest of the classes went on with a familiar monotony. At the end of the day, John said goodbye with a quick kiss on the cheek and ran off to work, leaving me there, my mind gnawing at me with frustration. I think it was even worse to receive these small, hasty gestures than to have no contact with him at all. The scent his affection left in me and the fragments of taste from his lips only made me despair for him even more, giving me the feeling that my body was always sick and that he was the cure that escaped my hands.

But I took a deep breath, trying to think of other things, and finally left. On the subway, I decided to read Dark Angel's response to my email.

"Black Rose,

I'm sorry you lost your job. But I'm glad you're okay. If it wasn't your dream job, who knows, maybe it was a door opening to finding something you really love? Something related to art, maybe?

Speaking of art, I saw your picture on the blog. Stunning! I was literally speechless as I admired your beautiful work. The way you work with the details gives the impression that what you see is a photo, given the realistic element of the painting, but at the same time, it is possible to detect the unreality there, as if the truth went much further than the real world. Your truth, I mean. Anyway, I'm not sure if what I'm saying makes any sense, but the point is that I really liked your work and I think it belongs in a gallery or a museum.

I'm flattered to know that I gave you the motivation to keep producing, but don't forget it wasn't much more than that: just a little push. You are the one who holds the talent and the inspiration. I hope you never stop creating. The world needs artists.

Regarding insomnia, I had to resort to medication, too, for a long time. But then I gradually left them until I didn't need them anymore. Nowadays, a glass of hot milk and a boring movie are enough to make me fall asleep.

I don't think I'll start a revolution in my work by wearing more colorful clothes, but to be honest, I'm seriously thinking about it. With so many colors in this world, so many patterns, why stick to just black, brown, navy blue, right? Maybe I'll do some shopping this weekend. Perhaps after my visit to the gallery? I will definitely be inspired.

I guess I don't want to be a refined adult then. Do you know how much work it takes to paint a fence white? No, thanks.

Xoxo,

Dark Angel"

As always, his message appeased that something that was agonizing me. I managed to get John out of my head and fill it with just the flavors of Dark Angel's appreciation for my painting—which made my soul so happy that I couldn't stop smiling. I'm sure the people around me in that train thought I was crazy. No one smiles alone in the middle of the day in New York City. But as a good resident of a large metropolis, I had long mastered the art of ignoring such trifles.

I decided to answer him later. I wanted to stop by the store, buy ingredients to make dinner for Kat—since that marriage proposal had been made, and I had no idea how it went but I assumed not very well. I decided I would do a Mexican night with guacamole and nachos and margaritas. It was her favorite cuisine. And in case she didn't want to talk, I thought we could watch a movie together. There's nothing like stepping out of reality for a moment to gain perspective or, at worst, distract yourself a little.

My visit to the grocery store was quick. Without a job, I couldn't afford to wander the aisles and be tempted to buy things I didn't need. After that, I went to a liquor store to get tequila for the drinks I planned to make later. This was an inconvenience in that country. You couldn't buy alcoholic beverages everywhere, like in Brazil. Arms full of bags, then, I walked a few blocks to my apartment. When I got home, I left the groceries in the kitchen and went to my room to put my purse away. There, I came across my painting on the wall. I smiled. I quickly checked my blog and saw a single comment on the posted photo. It was from Dark Angel, of course. It said:

"As always, I am not shocked to be surprised by a work of yours of such beauty and essence. Never stop creating. Never fail to show your art to the world.
Dark Angel"

It was, for me, absurd how this being, in a way, ethereal, could make my life so happy. I wanted to answer him right away, but something else came over me—like a physical urge or I don't know what. I took another one of the blank canvases I had bought and put it on my study desk, along with the paints and brushes. I sat across from them.

As it happened when I was in this state of...inspiration? I let my fingers instinctively seek out the colors. I watched my hand dip the brush into the red paint, begin to brush fluidly across the canvas, then move into shades of yellow, brown, black, and beige. With precision and spontaneity, my painting gradually took shape. I saw on that canvas the slightly distorted image of a female figure surrounded by flames. She was not, however, afraid. The fire wasn't part of her, but it belonged to her world and they coexisted, as it should be.

After it was over, I was tired and satisfied. Slowly, contrary to the previous eagerness, I closed the paint pots, washed the brushes, put away all the supplies. Then I walked to the bathroom, still taking my time, feeling my feet touch the floor with each step. I meant to take a quick shower, but instead, I decided to take a bath. Almost every home in America had a bathtub, but it was funny how little it was used. As water gushed out to fill it, I went into the kitchen and poured myself a glass of red wine. I went back to the bathroom, threw some bath salts that belonged to Kat into the water, put a selection of songs on my phone (from bossa nova to classical music), and plunged into the lull of that moment.

I don't know how long I stayed there, sipping my wine, listening to songs that transported me to other times and other places, some of which I hadn't even been to, and feeling the salts walk through my body covered by the waters, but when I decided that the bath was finished, I felt extremely refreshed. With a towel wrapped around my body, I looked quickly in the bathroom mirror, and my eyes looked like they belonged to someone who had found whatever it is that all people in this world are looking for. I was pure calm. A breath.

I got out of the bathroom, put on some comfortable clothes, and went to the kitchen to start making dinner, as Kat would be home in a few hours. The music coming from my cell phone was still playing and I let the melodies penetrate my being as I cooked. Masterfully accompanying the sounds were the aromas that originated from spices and herbs and seasonings. The world was suddenly nothing more than an ocean of senses. My hands were touching the rustic ingredients that would soon, like a miracle, become a meal. My nose could smell the mixture of scents. My ears welcomed the combination of the music and the sounds produced by the oil that sautéed meat and onions. My eyes saw the transformation of raw elements into edible food. And finally, my mouth felt the flavors that came with each step of that extraordinary experience.

At one point, everything was done. I put the food on the table with the plates and cutlery laid out simply and went to make the margaritas. As I mixed the drink in a pitcher, I heard the door open and concluded that Kat was home. I heard her footsteps to the couch and when she tossed her bag somewhere and kicked off her shoes. Then I heard her coming towards the kitchen. She, surprised, looked to me and to the table, alternately.

"Hey, what's all this?" she asked.

"I hope you don't mind, but I thought we could have a fun night and eat dinner together."

She smiled enthusiastically and moved closer to the table, examining the food while I finished making the drink. I poured the margarita into two pre-prepared glasses with salt around the edges, in a very traditional way, and offered one of them to Kat. She picked up her drink and took a sip.

"Yum, delicious!"

I smiled and drank some of mine too. The bitter-sweet taste kind of tickled the roof of my mouth. She continued to speak, as we both sat at the table.

"Thank you so much! Everything looks delicious. But why did you decide to do this?"

"I thought you might want to talk about your date with Jordan. I didn't get a chance to ask you how it went and how you're feeling."

Kat's expression suddenly changed to something that looked like a mixture of sadness and resignation. She took another sip of her drink, helped herself to a nacho, and, after eating, finally replied, "I was wrong. He didn't ask me to marry him."

I looked at her, waiting for what she would say next. She ate some more and took a generous swig of the margarita before continuing to speak. I also started snacking on the food while listening to her.

"He got a job offer in California. And, well... he took it. Dinner was to tell me he's moving across the country."

"I'm sorry, Kat."

"Yeah, me too. I didn't understand why he couldn't have told me that while we were at his apartment or here or anywhere else. He made me..." She paused and sipped the last of the margarita in her glass. I got up to get the pitcher from the counter and refilled it. "He made me consider the possibility of marrying him. And yes, I know what I said about that before, but as I was sitting across from him in that fancy restaurant, my mind went to a future that...well, isn't going to happen anyway."

I tried to give her some comfort through a friendly look, as I didn't know what to say to her that would help in any way.

"I was so stupid to let myself get involved like that with someone like him. From the beginning, we had this understanding that it wasn't and never would be something serious and, even so, I plunged into this relationship without even realizing it."

"You weren't stupid, Kat. These things are not under our control. I believe that every experience we go through is never a total waste of time. You can always learn something and make the best of it."

She smiled sadly and nodded.

"You're right."

"What happened after he told you he was leaving?"

"Nothing. I said I would miss him, wished him good luck. We finished eating, and he brought me home."

She downed the rest of the margarita in her glass and handed it to me as if asking for more. I served her the drink.

"When will he move?" I asked.

"In two weeks. Can you believe he had the nerve to say we could spend this time together? He wanted, no joke, for me to help him pack for the trip."

Kat took another sip of her drink and I started to get a little worried. If she got drunk, the next day would be hard to take.

"Do you have to work tomorrow?" I wanted to make sure she wouldn't miss a job because of a hangover.

"Yes, but only in the evening. I'm going to photograph an engagement party."

Her tone held a sad irony and she drank again. I tried to get her to eat some more, but she no longer seemed interested in the food. The rest of the night was bathed in more margaritas and her lamentation. We didn't get to see a movie, as she got too drunk to even sit on the couch. So I put her to bed, a glass of water on her nightstand and a bucket on the floor in case she woke up to vomit.

After cleaning the kitchen and putting away the leftover food, I went to bed myself. I kept thinking about the last time I'd had my heart broken by a man. At the time I was, as Kat is now, a mess in human form—even worse, in fact. We'd dated for three years and I'd clung to him as one clings to a distant hope. We had been in a codependent relationship until the day he broke free—even though I wasn't free myself. I remember feeling as if the whole world was collapsing on my shoulders, an impossible weight to carry with my eighteen years of age—or so it seemed at the time.

I chased away the memory then. It didn't hurt anymore, but it reminded me of a Clara that my current self tried to forget at all costs. I took out my cell phone to reread Dark Angel's comment, and also his email, which I decided to respond to. Suddenly, as I immersed myself in that reading, the rest of the world disappeared. I didn't think about Kat or John or my past or my present anymore. There, I was Black Rose, just an artist. An artist who had found a dear friend to share her work with. And she was happy. Her life was complete. She wrote back to him.

"Dark Angel,

I would love for my job loss to be just a small adversity that, in the end, would lead me to find my dream job, but I don't think that's the case at the moment. Either way, I appreciate the sympathy.

I just read your comment on the blog and I am extremely happy that you liked my work so much. To tell you the truth, if I can take off the mask of modesty for a moment, I am quite proud of my painting. And I really liked your interpretation of it. You have an amazing eye for art. As for my painting belonging to a museum or gallery, I don't know if that's true, but I would love an exhibition that goes beyond the internet.

You didn't just give me a "push" to continue producing. You're pretty much the only person I share my art with, and knowing that you appreciate it makes me want to work on it even more. The world needs people who make art, yes, but it also needs people who consume, respect, and esteem this art. Without you, I'm nothing as an artist.

Well, I'm glad you don't need sleeping pills anymore. I find this thing about milk helping people sleep very funny, but whatever helps...

I think this idea of wearing more colorful clothes is fantastic. I don't know why society equates seriousness with darkness (at least in the wardrobe). Your weekend will be inspired for sure. I'm excited for you! I can't wait to find out how it went.

Yeah, being a refined adult really takes work. I'd rather not even try. No white fences—just good old-fashioned existential crises, alcohol, and listening to bad music without judgment.

Hope the next few days are great!

Xoxo,
Black Rose"

After sending the message, in my slight drunkenness from the margaritas, I couldn't resist letting my Dark Angel fantasies take over my thoughts: art, and flirtation, and refinement, and complexity. My mind flew away with him because I knew these daydreams would never be more than that. I felt safe in creating a make-believe world with my virtual friend, as I was protected by my cell phone or computer screen, from where he would never leave.

⇒⇒⇒ ⇐⇐⇐

The next day dragged on without much happening. I woke up late and looked at some job positions online without much effort because I was slightly hungover. And I took advantage of the forced time off to clean the apartment. Kat was a mess, and if it was up to her, the place would end up being devoured by the chaos of disorder and rot. I tried not to make too much noise as I cleaned so I wouldn't wake her, though I doubted she'd get out of bed anytime soon after her drunkenness from the night before.

After cleaning, I took a shower and then lay down on the couch in the living room with the computer.

I looked again at my blog and my email, but there was nothing new. Or rather, nothing that Dark Angel had sent. I decided to work a little on college stuff. I made a list of topics that could be part of my thesis, even though I didn't have to turn it in for two more years—just because. I thought of John too. I couldn't wait for the weekend. The time I had with him in school interrupted by classes and by his busy job didn't even come close to satisfying me. Two days from now, I would have him all to myself, and just that thought left me in a state of euphoria.

As my thoughts raced over all these things of life, I heard a noise coming from Kat's room. After a few minutes, she appeared in the living room.

"Good morning!" she said in a husky voice, followed by a yawn.

"Good morning," I replied. "How are you? Did you sleep well?"

She plopped down on the couch and emitted what sounded like the whimper of some wounded animal. I moved my legs to give her more space, and she stretched for a long time before answering me. "I slept like a rock until I woke up around two in the morning and threw up everything I ever ate and drank in my entire life."

My face contorted into an expression of solidarity.

"Thanks for the bucket, by the way," she continued, "and as for how I am now, well... my head hurts and the whole apartment seems to be spinning. Not to mention the moral hangover, but I'll be fine."

"Hope you feel better soon. There's coffee in the kitchen and aspirin in the bathroom cabinet. And you should eat something greasy, it helps with the hangover. And, of course, plenty of water."

"Thank you, Clara. And for yesterday, too. Sorry I drank more than I should have."

"Now, you have nothing to apologize for. But next time, maybe I'll make pineapple juice instead of margaritas."

She laughed and threw a pillow in my direction. Then she went to the kitchen, and I went back to my college stuff, but only for a moment. I thought of John again. Closing my eyes, I could, at that very moment, smell the scent that emanated from him, and that alone made my knees weak, so much so that I had to stretch them out on the couch to make sure they were still there. I shook my head as if to send away the thought, but it insisted on coming back and reigning again, bordering on obsession.

Kat came back from the kitchen with a cup of coffee and a slice of toast. She sat in the armchair next to the sofa I was on. I put the computer aside for a bit.

"Feeling a little better?" I asked her.

She shrugged her shoulders and replied. "Yeah, I think so. Nothing like a good coffee, right?"

"Yes, that's true."

I went back to my computer, an article about... (what was it about?) as she ate her breakfast in silence. When finished, Kat turned to me again.

"How's your life going?"

I closed the computer and returned my gaze to her once more.

"Um... it's okay. I'm already looking for a new job."

"Oh, good, good. By the way, I was going to tell you that I have a friend who might need a waitress for the night shift at the restaurant he manages. I can arrange an interview for you."

"Oh, thanks, but I'm looking for a nanny job right now. I think my waitress days are gone."

"Ah, okay. Well, if I know of anyone who needs a nanny, I'll let you know. Not that I know a lot of people with kids, but you never know."

"Thank you."

"And how's school?"

"Oh, it's going well. You know, the usual."

"Yeah, yeah..." She hesitated for a moment, taking a sip of her coffee, but then continued. "What about your dating life? You didn't tell me about that date with the guy from college. And I... I know I've been pretty self-centered, just talking about my life and all, but I want to know about you."

"Oh, the date was very good. In fact, we have another one this weekend."

She smiled enthusiastically as I spoke.

"Wow, such a quick second date. How exciting!"

I smiled too.

"Yes, I'm excited."

"My God, Clara, you're the vaguest person I've ever met. It takes a lot of squeezing for more accurate information." She chuckled before continuing. "Tell me more: how is he, how are you feeling? Have you guys kissed?"

I chuckled discreetly with her.

"Sorry, I don't know why I always do this. Well, where do I start? He works in finance, but also teaches music as a volunteer. He's handsome, charming, intelligent, and has a hint of mystery that fascinates me. And yes, we kissed."

"How was the kiss?" Her voice held an excited fervor.

I smiled to myself as I thought of John's lips against mine and all the sensations my body had experienced from such an intimate gesture.

"It was amazing. One of the best I've ever had."

Kat jumped onto the couch next to me.

"I'm so happy for you!"

"Thank you. I don't want to get too carried away, because you never know with men, but at the same time, I can't help myself when I'm around him. And, to be honest, not even when I'm just thinking about him."

"You're in love!"

My smile suddenly faded.

"No, I wouldn't use the words 'in love.' I barely know him. We just went out for coffee and then a few beers, and we never really talk in school."

She shrugged her shoulders condescendingly as she spoke. "You can say that to yourself, but to me, you sound like someone who is falling for this guy."

After that, she went to her room—the audacity of leaving me alone with my...conflicting thoughts? No, it was not what she thought, for sure. Although it might seem so. But the obvious: it is clear that being alone in a new country, any sensation would have a gigantic proportion. Lonely as I felt, evidently the attention of an attractive man would make me feel... even a virtual stranger made me feel... things. Anyone in my place would have similar experiences. Of course.

I decided to get back to studying—to force myself to be productive, to not think—which I did from my room so I wouldn't be interrupted by Kat. I finally managed to get the thoughts that haunted me out of my head. It was already nighttime when I decided to turn off the computer. Before doing so, however, I checked my email once more, but there was no message from him. I decided to distract myself with a book that I had started to read almost a month ago but hadn't managed to finish yet. I went to get it from the drawer of my study desk and came across the picture I had painted earlier lying there. I had completely forgotten about it (I wondered how). It was beautiful. I decided to call it "Woman in Flames." I hung it on the wall next to that first painting.

I took my book from the drawer, but before starting to read, I took a long look at my paintings. They made me proud of who I was. They were born of me. And that was an incredible thing. And an unbelievable thing. I myself didn't know how the process of creating them happened. I just painted. It was simple, but as complex as it could be. I wondered if it was like that for every artist. Probably not. But I thought some would be able to understand me, no doubt.

I dove into my book after the daydreams and stayed there until the words began to shuffle across the pages and the sentences stopped making sense. It was sleep that called me to its arms. I closed the book, set up an alarm on my phone, and fell asleep quickly. I entered a deep, dreamless somnolence state that took me to the nothingness so longed for by those who perish.

W aking up to the sound of my alarm, which seemed distant and unrecognizable for a good few seconds, I felt like I had just fallen asleep, and, at the same time, it seemed as if I had slept for days on end. I got up then and got ready for class. It was Friday, and the possibilities of the weekend were becoming more and more real. I mentally prepared myself for another morning of little contact with John, but, knowing that it would be the last one that week, everything was easier.

On the subway on my way to school, I checked my email one more time, hoping to see a response from Dark Angel, but again, there was nothing. Although I didn't want to admit it, his absence, even though it wasn't that long, was making me uneasy. I was suddenly afraid of losing my virtual friend. Without him, my art would become empty and meaningless. And I would go back to being, too, empty and meaningless. But, however... he was probably busy with work. Or with life. After all, he certainly had a (life) outside the internet.

I arrived at college early. It was cold that day, so I entered the building and sat on one of the benches in the entrance hall. Two or three more people were there, and among them, I recognized Alex, the girl who'd lent me her makeup. She was sitting in front of me across the lobby, fiddling with her cell phone. She looked up for a second and, seeing me, smiled in greeting. I smiled back and decided to go to her.

"Good morning," I greeted her as I sat down beside her. She put the phone away and turned to me.

"Good morning. Clara, right?"

"That's right. And you are Alex."

"Yeah."

We looked at each other, still smiling, for a little while in a slightly awkward silence. Then, she broke the stillness.

"You're early today."

"Yeah, I woke up on time today, and the subway was weirdly fast this morning. You're early too."

Truisms.

"Yeah, I always get here around this time. I live in Brooklyn, so if I don't leave the house very early, I end up being late."

"Oh, I see."

Once again, we entered an almost withdrawn silence. I was terrible with words, and Alex seemed to suffer from the same ailment. Or maybe she was just shy. Or just quiet. I tried to think of something we could talk about.

"So, you study Creative Writing. Who is your favorite author?"

Her face seemed to light up for a moment. I sensed that the topic was one of her favorites. She responded to my question almost immediately.

"Poe. Edgar Allan Poe. Do you know him?"

"I do, yes. I read a few short stories when I was a teenager, and I remember liking them a lot."

"He's awesome! His theme is kind of dark, but I really like his gothic style, you know?"

"I do. It was my favorite when I was a teenager. I liked Goethe, Lord Byron, and some Brazilian authors with a similar style."

"Brazilian authors? How peculiar! Is your family from Brazil?"

"I am, actually. I moved here not long ago."

"I was detecting a bit of an accent. But your English is great, I would never have thought you just got here."

"Thank you."

We continued talking for quite some time. I told her a little about my life in Brazil and the authors I liked. She jotted down some names to look up English translations. We talked about literature almost the entire time. She told me that she read everything she could when she was a child and had always known that she wanted to be a writer when she grew up. Alex was someone to be admired. She had never even thought about doing things other than steps towards achieving her dreams. Even the jobs she'd had, she saw as opportunities to develop characters, write poems, and all that.

We engaged in conversation in such a way that I didn't notice when John entered the building. I only did when he was very close in front of us. I took my gaze to him and greeted him with a smile, which was immediately responded to with the same gesture. I got up, and we exchanged a quick hug. He was, once again, holding two cups of coffee and offered me one. I thanked him. He then looked at Alex and said hi. I realized I hadn't introduced them.

"Oh, sorry," I started to say, looking back and forth between the two of them. "John, this is Alex. Alex, this is John. He's in my class."

Alex held out her hand, which John politely took.

"Nice to meet you," she said softly, with distinct shyness.

"Nice to meet you too," he replied politely.

"Well, I'm going to my classroom," Alex continued, her gaze lowered. "I'll talk to you later, Clara."

We said goodbye, and John sat next to me, where she had been before. He was strangely smiley that morning. He wore a plaid shirt under his usual leather jacket and pale blue jeans that made him incredibly tempting. As I was drinking my coffee, he began to speak.

"I can't believe today is finally Friday! This week has been extremely difficult at work. I barely have time to breathe."

"Well," I replied, "at least it helps the time go by more quickly."

"That's what you'd think, but to me, it feels like these days are taking forever to end. But that probably has to do with my anticipation for the weekend."

I was glad to know that I wasn't alone in my longing for the next few days.

"I can't wait either," I replied, and after that, the stillness took over. We were more and more comfortable with the silence when together. We just sat there drinking our coffees until it was time for classes to start.

The morning passed quickly and calmly. At the end of class, once again, John told me goodbye in a hurry, but with the promise of seeing each other soon. Otherwise, everything went according to the daily routine. On the way home, I was disappointed again that I still hadn't had any response from Dark

Angel. However, I had instead received an email with a job offer. It was to take care of a baby. The mom asked me to call her as soon as possible, which I did when I got home, and we set up an interview for the following week.

After that, with no work and no chores, I felt lost in my apartment. I didn't know what to do with myself. I thought about painting but didn't find the disposition to do so. Although I didn't want to admit it, the distant thought of the possibility that I had lost my virtual friend gave me a feeling that there was no point in venturing out to start a new painting. I could sit on the couch and finish my book, but I didn't feel like that either. In the end, giving up, I turned on the TV and entertained myself there, giving my mind the gift of not having to think for endless hours.

I saw Kat come home and then leave again. It was Friday, and my roommate refused to do anything other than enjoy the New York night. I, on the other hand, put on my pajamas and went back to numbing myself with the television until I fell asleep right there on the couch. I dreamed of the days to come. But in the dream, it wasn't John I was dating, it was Dark Angel. And we were not in the United States, but on some island that had not yet been discovered by humans. We ate pears and drank water from the river. And then we made love on the sands of the beach, but in an almost incorporeal way, without really touching each other, although all the sensations were present with greater intensity than usual.

I was suddenly awakened by a loud noise that seemed to be right next to my ear. Still disoriented, I came across Kat and a guy I'd never seen before trying to contain a laugh. Upon realizing that I had woken up, my roommate burst out laughing and then said, in a clearly intoxicated voice, "Sorry, Clara, my love. I dropped the lamp."

The two laughed again as if the funniest thing in the world had happened.

"No problem," I replied, getting up from the couch to go to my room. From inside, I heard the two of them heading to her room, not before bumping into half the furniture.

Despite the noise, I went back to sleep quickly. I had no more dreams about my virtual friend and woke up again only the next day. It was still early; the sun gave timid signs of waking up. I went to the kitchen, made some coffee. I checked my social media and my emails and looked at the news of the day. Wars, hunger, fascism. It was a lot for a Saturday morning. I looked out the kitchen window, and the city was sunny at last. I took the opportunity to focus on that—and conscious alienation helped me find beauty in the world.

Several hours later, which I used to enjoy nothingness, I heard Kat's bedroom door open. I turned to greet her but ran into the man from last night in his underwear, who told me a casual "good morning." I answered him politely and turned to myself again. I heard him going to the bathroom and then to the kitchen, pouring himself some coffee and opening doors and drawers. Kat never let anyone stay overnight, except for Jordan, and I figured then that she was having some sort of reaction to her recent heartbreak.

When I realized that her "friend" was making eggs for breakfast, I decided to go for a walk. It was a beautiful day, and I had no desire to interact with a stranger that morning. I changed quickly, grabbed my purse, and left the house, not sure what I was going to do or where I was going to go. As I walked aimlessly down the street, without realizing it, I did that thing of observing art in everyday life. The colors, the shadings and geometric shapes, the patterns on the clothes, and the designs on the shop windows jumped to my eyes effortlessly. I thought of Dark Angel again, of course. And in all those little things that we shared, that made our relationship expand from the virtual world. What I saw and felt now was part of the real world. And the dream from the night before—it also belonged to reality. And these worlds of "truth" and "almost-truth" mixed together, forming a kind of a blur of thoughts.

⇢⇢⇢⇉ ⇇⇇⇇⇠

O n my aimless walk, I ended up finding a small boutique around some corner. I stopped to look at the window. One of the mannequins was wearing a dress very similar to one that belonged to Kat. The look was completed by colorful accessories, which also very much resembled her style. I entered the store on an impulse and ended up buying a purse and sunglasses—the ones in the window—as a birthday present for my friend. Happy with the acquisitions, I returned to my walk.

The journey ended up taking me to a part of the neighborhood I didn't know yet. It was a little less busy. I saw some children playing in the street, a woman pushing a baby stroller, and a couple walking a dog. Yet another big-city contrast; and how many it had! I smiled at life on that sunny morning, feeling like I was floating, untouched by the chaos of everyday life. While enjoying that state of pleasure, I felt my cell phone vibrate in my purse. I had forgotten about that little device that was such a part of my life—how? I picked it up to see what notification woke me up, thinking it might be an email from my dark angel. Instead, it was a text message from John.

"Hey, good morning! Can I drop by to pick you up at seven tonight?"

It was funny. In the days leading up to Saturday, I was in such a state of excitement about our date that I could barely concentrate on the small tasks of daily life. And now that the day had come, that craving was almost completely gone. I was still excited, of course, but nothing like my previous sensations. I replied.

"Good morning! Seven sounds great."

So I started walking back home. On arriving there, I found Kat sitting on the couch, a bag of potato chips in her hand and the television on. Her "friend" was gone, apparently. I said a quick "hello" and went to my room to drop off the bag with her gifts. I went back into the living room and sat with her, watching what looked like a new reality show—something about rich teenagers partying on their boats, or the dangers of teenage sex, or both.

I didn't pay much attention, spending more time on my phone than on TV, but she seemed very interested. When the show went to commercials, she turned down the volume and said, "Sorry about the guy this morning."

I put my phone aside and replied. "It's all right. Who was he, anyway?"

"Friend of a friend. He was at the bar yesterday with the guys. Peter something."

I nodded. She continued.

"You know I don't like them spending the night, but I ended up falling asleep last night, and when I woke up, he was in the kitchen eating."

"It's not a problem, really."

We returned to the silence, broken only by the TV. I was fiddling with my cell phone again, and I thought the matter was closed when she spoke once more.

"Clara, I don't want you to think I'm one of those women who hook up with a lot of different guys."

I intriguingly looked at her.

"What's wrong with women who date too many guys?" I asked.

She looked confused for a moment, and then replied. "Nothing, that's not what I meant."

I looked at her, waiting for her to continue, but she didn't. I then said, "Kat, you're upset about Jordan. I understand your reaction. Drinking, having sex, trying to have a little fun to get him out of your head, it's all normal and super acceptable. And even if you hadn't gone through any of this, I would never judge you for doing as you please with your own body."

She looked thoughtful for a few seconds but just nodded in agreement. We spent some more time there, our voices hushed, the volume of the television interrupting the small discomfort of her internalized sexism. Then she went to pack her things—Kat was going to her parent's house in New Jersey. And I would have the apartment all to myself, a circumstance I liked. I got along well with her, and we lived together without major problems, but I liked the prospect of being alone, if only for one night.

I had butterflies, the ones talked about in pop culture, when I got the text message that John was in front of the building—I'm sure they were circling somewhere in my guts, eating me up inside, perhaps. I buzzed him in and gave him my apartment number. A few minutes later, I heard his knock on the door. In an uproar now, they (the butterflies) glided towards my heart. I opened the door to receive him. He was wearing a light-blue T-shirt and dark jeans. He didn't have his leather jacket on this time; instead, he held a denim coat in his hands.

I greeted him with a kiss on the cheek and led him inside. He looked around quickly and said, probably out of politeness, "Nice place."

"Thanks. Do you want to sit down, have a drink?"

"Sure. Thank you."

He sat on the couch, and I went into the kitchen to open a bottle of wine. I offered him a glass, which he took, thanking me again. All very clean, full of good manners, please, and thank you. I sat beside him, and we both sipped our wine.

"You look beautiful," he said after placing the glass on the coffee table, looking at me intently. I really did, with my makeup and my curled hair and my high heels, which I never wore, but I thought the occasion deserved the extra effort.

"Thank you. So do you."

We looked at each other for a few moments without saying anything until he broke the silence once more.

"Do you live alone?"

"No, but my roommate is out of town this weekend."

He nodded and went back to sipping his wine. I did the same.

"What are the plans for tonight?" I asked at one point.

"I made dinner reservations at an Italian place that I really like. Then we can have a few drinks at the Plaza bar."

The Plaza was a mega luxury hotel in the city. I smiled at him. "Sounds great."

We stayed there a while longer, drinking the wine and talking about unimportant things. The pleasant warmth of the drink began to make itself present in my body, and the conversation became more fluid. We had another glass each, and then we left. He asked for a car via app, and in less than twenty minutes, we were there. The restaurant was very beautiful. You could see that it was an elegant place, but at the same time, the atmosphere emanated a cozy feeling—which gave me the (false?) impression of belonging.

We sat at a table in the far corner—which was good, as the place was full. Amidst the classical music playing in the background, the voices of the people around us, some very loud, made communication a little difficult. But nevertheless, we managed to talk.

"I hope you like the place," John said once we were seated.

"I already do," I replied, smiling. "There's a cozy atmosphere here."

"The food is delicious, too. I recommend the pesto ravioli."

I opened the menu, scanned the dishes quickly, already half-knowing that I would end up accepting his recommendation—a statement of trust. A waiter came to our table, read the night's specials, full of names of things I didn't know. John ordered a wine bottle and an appetizer while I sipped my water, which, like most restaurants in that country, came without us having asked. A basket of bread also rested in the center of the table; courtesies—bread and water—for the privileged. Of course.

We talked a little about the frivolities of life. Each other's company, in itself, already brought a pleasant feeling to the aura of the encounter. And the freedom to laugh and to talk banalities without worrying was a gift I enjoyed fully—every second of it. We were interrupted by the waiter, who brought us our wine. He poured some of it into John's glass, who tasted it and nodded. Only then were we properly served.

I tasted some of my wine. The acrid yet sweet flavor of Bacchus's drink gently descended into my throat, adding to the delight of the evening. He also took a sip.

"Excellent choice," I exclaimed.

"I'm glad you like it. I don't know much about wine, to be honest, but this is my favorite."

As he spoke, I noticed a certain gleam in his eyes. I couldn't quite identify what was that glint that emanated from him, but it was certainly there. That aspect of John fascinated me. It was possible to detect something in him, but I could never guess what it was—even though that certain thing was so evidently there. It was frustrating, but also very seductive. It made me want to dive deeper into his waters to finally discover his mysteries, even if there could also be danger in those depths. At that moment, however, I just wanted to venture further and further into that man, despite the fear that hovered around my will.

We continued to drink our wine, which went from one glass to two, three, a bottle. Our meal was a feast of flavors, which we shared and enjoyed with great pleasure. The conversation moved into deeper fields at one point. The inhibition that, to a certain degree, was a personality trait for both of us, completely disappeared and gave way to spontaneity.

"I grew up in a poor family." The words left my lips at some random instant of the evening. "But real 'poor,' not America's 'poor.'"

"What do you mean? There are poor people here."

"Yes, yes, but the poor here have cars and cell phones and cable. I didn't have much else to eat besides rice and beans sometimes. But I'm being unfair. There are people who don't even have that."

John looked at me with a mixture of empathy and admiration.

"But look at you today," he said, his voice slightly altered by the wine, as I'm sure mine was too.

"That's right," I replied. "I'm living the American dream."

We both burst out laughing and then he continued.

"But seriously, you made it out of your country and are now getting your Master's. Be proud of yourself."

"I am. Thank you."

Smiling at each other, we sipped some more wine and he went on.

"My parents had money when I was growing up. We traveled every year, and I had all the toys I wanted. But they didn't speak to each other. Well, sometimes, but it was just to yell."

"I'm sorry."

"Oh, it's all right! They ended up getting divorced as soon as I left home for college. I think they didn't do it before because of me."

"It's bizarre how parents think that by not separating, they'll cause less pain when the opposite is so true."

"Yeah..."

We stayed there for a few more minutes. We had already finished our dinner, and the waiter brought us the check. I mean, he brought it to John, of course. But I was faster and caught it. He wanted to pay, obviously, and I could argue the systemic issue that made him feel that obligation, but oh, the wine and my desire to have him without the chains of non-alienation made the simplest explanation come out of my mouth.

"You always pay for everything."

John got up from his chair and offered me his arm. Strong—I felt small. And I was dizzier than I had imagined. Weak. He let me lean on his shoulder to walk better. We went out of the restaurant to wait for a taxi. The evening air had cooled; I put on my jacket. He was still holding his, not seeming to be bothered by the icy breath coming from who-knows where. We didn't have to wait long. A cab stopped a few minutes after we got out, and we hurried to get in.

Without having arranged it with John, I gave my address to the driver. We couldn't (or I couldn't) drink more, and I assumed we'd skip going to the Plaza. And anyway, I assumed he wanted to accompany me home. Assumptions... just mine?—but which he did not oppose. As soon as we were settled in the car and the man started driving, John surprised me with a kiss. In shock at the sudden gesture, I didn't react at first, only slowly surrendering to his arms. That kiss wasn't tender and romantic; there was urgency, hunger. His lips pressed against mine greedily, and his arms held me tightly. I responded with the same eagerness, sensations taking over the center of my universe.

The kiss must have not lasted that long, but it felt like Earth's lifetime had passed. After, John looked at me with tenderness, although not hiding the desire that was also in him, and whispered in my ear.

"I love kissing you."

His murmur seemed to travel through my body, leaving a trail of goosebumps wherever it went. Breathless, I just smiled at him in response. Then I pulled his head against mine and we kissed once again—with passion. As our lips and our tongues intertwined, my hand, still on the back of his head, began to play with his hair while the other leaned on the car seat. And John alternated caresses through my hair, my face, arms, and waist. With some hesitation, slowly, I felt one of his hands sliding to my thigh. In response, I lightly bit his lip. He then put some pressure on the touch, squeezing me lustfully. I let my body be taken over by my senses, forgetting where I was and even who I was. All that mattered in that instant were the sensations my flesh gave me.

We stopped suddenly when we felt that the car had stopped moving. We were parked in front of my building. John paid the taxi driver and we got out. I didn't have to ask him if he wanted to come in. Automatically, in silent agreement, he just followed me as I opened the gate and walked toward the elevator. Inside of it (ah, the cliché!), we started the caresses again. This time, with the full certainty that we were on the same page, John was more fearless in his moves. His hand gripped my thigh tightly now, helped by the slit in my skirt, and from there, he ventured to caress my buttocks. I could barely breathe. I responded to his advances with hoarse groans and squeezed his arms tightly.

The elevator stopped and—I don't know how, as my legs were barely obeying me—I walked to my apartment door, followed by him. As soon as we entered, barely closing the door behind us, we continued to kiss. I threw my bag on the floor and took off my jacket, putting my arms around his shoulders. John threw his jacket on the floor too, hugged me around the waist. Now protected by the privacy of those walls, there were no more restrained gestures. His hands roamed over every inch of my body with haste and anxiety. He ended up lifting me off the floor, and I put my legs around him. Totally surrendered to his arms, I let him lead me to my bedroom.

Once inside, John carefully placed me on the bed and lay there with me, kissing me again, this time a little more calmly. The rush seemed to have disappeared. He slowly removed my clothes, then his own, and gazed at me for a moment, as if in front of a work of art in a museum. Then he went back to touching and kissing and gesturing. Our sweat and fluids and groans mixed together as if they were all part of one body. And as part of a process as natural as time, John protected himself and invaded me, slowly at first, then increasing his pace as the next few seconds demanded. And I let my body experience the graduation of pleasure that eventually turned into the contraction of extreme satisfaction.

I fell asleep in John's arms. It was a deep sleep that came over me as if I was suddenly free of whatever longings life brought as part of its bargain. The comfort of that embrace was like nothing I had ever experienced, and even though we were squashed together in my single bed, I had never felt such comfort.

When I woke up, however, I was alone. I slowly opened my eyes and, little by little, remembered reality—dinner, wine, enjoyment... John; where would he be? I yawned openly, stretched my arms, turned around between the sheets, feeling his scent fill my nostrils. Silence surrounded the apartment; for a moment I thought he was gone. However, the same second the thought crossed my mind, John opened my bedroom door. Relief. He was wearing yesterday's pants and carrying two cups of coffee in his hands. He offered me one, kissed my forehead, and said, "Good morning! I hope you don't mind, but I got up early and used your coffee maker."

I smiled and, after yawning again, replied, "No problem, make yourself at home. Thank you for the coffee."

I sat up to take the cup he gave me. The sheet covering me slid down, revealing my bare breasts. I took a generous sip of my coffee as John sat down next to me. He looked around for a moment and his gaze lingered on the two paintings above my bed.

"Very beautiful," he said at last.

"Thank you," I replied. "I painted them myself."

John looked up from the paintings to my face, surprised by the revelation. He was silent for a few seconds.

"I didn't know you painted. You're very talented!"

"Thank you."

So that was it. I expected him to have more to say, but the matter ended there. John busied himself with his coffee while leaning against the headboard, and I did the same. I got to thinking, even though I tried with all my might not to, of how Dark Angel would react if he was there—no generic compliments; art would take the environment as much as the oxygen we breathe. But... It was unfair of me to compare John to my virtual friend. It was very rare to find someone who was truly interested in the subject and had the artistic sensibility I wanted. He, John, after all, was who he was.

After coffee, he went to the shower. While he was there, I decided to make breakfast. A desire was born, to feed him, take care of him. I had *pão de queijo* dough, cheese rolls—a find—from a Brazilian store I discovered on the other side of town. And if there was one thing that was unanimous among the *gringos* I had met, it was the enchantment they shared with Brazilian flavors. Evidently. So, quickly, I mixed the dough with the requested ingredients (ah, the smell of home right in the preparation!), molded the balls, and put them in the oven. Then I set the table for breakfast—carefully, neatly. I felt like a good 50s housewife.

Satisfied, then, standing in my kitchen, wearing nothing but a robe and holding my coffee cup, occasionally raising it to my mouth, I found myself reminiscing about the night before—detail by detail. John certainly knew what he was doing, which was a pleasant surprise after a few disappointments in this area of life. Rare are the men who even pretend to be interested in a pleasure that isn't theirs. But it wasn't all his credit (of course). I had waited for that moment with so much eagerness and desire that I gave myself completely to the sensations. It was incredible the pleasure my body was able to give me. I loved it for that.

I woke up from my daydreams to the sound of the kitchen timer, indicating that the cheese rolls were ready. I took them out of the oven, and while they were still cooling in the pan, John appeared. He had a bath towel wrapped around his waist, and his wet hair spilled little drops of water down his bare shoulders. I smiled when I saw him. He smiled back, walked over to me, kissed me on the lips.

"Something smells good!" he said after, sitting down at the table and pouring himself a glass of orange juice that I had placed there.

"I made *pão de queijo.*" I said the name of the delicacy in Portuguese, then translated the meaning into English. "I hope you like it."

"How can someone not like bread made out of cheese? The smell is already amazing!"

I put the rolls in a bowl and then sat at the table with him. John, of course, fell in love with the food—which he expressed with words and the fact that he ate half of them. I laughed at his gluttony and for my contentment and pure happiness. What a delight to be alive and there—I wanted to pause time. But, oh, impossible, alas!

"What do you want to do today?" I asked. It didn't really matter to me, actually, as long as we were together.

"I can think of a few things..."

He then gave me a look full of bad intentions. I looked at him with false indignation for a moment, but then got up, went to him, and sat on his lap, putting my arms around his neck. He had a half-eaten roll in his hand, but he set it aside and turned his attention to me. We kissed. His caresses transported me to that world of sensations now known and appreciated. Sometimes uncontrollable laughter mingled with the sounds of my desire as his fingers tickled me. The caresses soon grew, and the kitchen floor was the stage for our second time. Again, irrevocable pleasure. Afterward, we were both lying on the cold floor, enjoying the calmness.

I finally got up, a little lost in the seconds (minutes?) that passed, followed by John. I went to the bathroom and he sat down at the table again, going back to the task of eating cheese rolls. I lingered in the shower, enjoying the warm water enveloping my body and cleaning off the fluids from earlier. When I left, I saw that he had cleaned the kitchen and washed the dishes and was sitting on the sofa in the living room, watching the news on TV. I thanked him casually, even though I wanted to give him the world in return, and went to get dressed.

Then, sitting next to him on the couch, we watched television together. Amidst the tragedies of world events, robberies, murders, abandonments, wars, one report or another brought a lightness to the soul of those who want to ignore the rottenness of a world that goes beyond the living room couch. They told, for example, the story of a little girl who raised funds for an NGO dedicated to psychologically treating children who had been bullied. They also spoke of a law in a faraway country that finally allowed people of the same gender to get married. I enthusiastically made comments about these stories with John, who responded accordingly but didn't seem very interested. Did he not understand the relevance of things? I forced myself not to be disappointed. Because I didn't want to be disappointed in that man. All I wanted was the good in him.

After watching TV for a while, now in total silence, we went out for lunch at a nearby diner. The day was beautiful. I ordered a salad and he had a sandwich—I missed the dirty premade meals from my proletarian days in São Paulo. We talked, once again, about the irrelevances of everyday life. The words were shallow, but the feelings I had as I heard them leave his lips were loaded with meaning, and that made perfect sense—and none at all, also, but I was starting to get used to these incongruities that coexisted inside me. And resignation was comfortable; I let it reign. John left me breathless even when he talked about the problem with not having a microwave in his office or how his friend had just bought a motorcycle of whatever kind or how he needed a new pair of running shoes. I gave great importance to what he said as if such matters were as relevant to me as they were to him.

After lunch, John said he had to go. My stomach twisted in contradiction. We returned to my apartment for a moment. I walked slowly, prolonging the moments, postponing the occasion to say goodbye, as if we would never see each other again as the ghost of the future suggests. He soon asked for a car on his phone, and we went down to wait for it. We didn't speak these last few minutes together. We just stood there, holding hands, looking either at the phone screen with the opened app or at the street in the direction the car would come from. I took that opportunity to memorize him with my senses: the smell, the touch... When we finally saw the vehicle, he kissed me superficially on the lips, and finally, we said goodbye. I watched the car turn the corner, disappearing into the distance, before heading back inside the building, alone once more.

When Kat got home that night, my brain was clear of any significant plots that were a part of my life as an individual or as a social being. My afternoon of watching sitcoms on TV took care of the thing; conscious alienation always worked. I chatted a little with my roommate about the weekend, telling her, without too much detail, how things went with John. She seemed excited for me and told me to invite him to her birthday party, which would be next week. Then she told me what it was like in New Jersey: family anecdotes and similarities. She seemed better now. We didn't bring up the subject of her ex, however, her countenance looked lighter. Nothing like walking away, sometimes.

That night, before going to sleep, I could no longer contain the course of my thoughts. I wondered where my dark angel was, who seemed to have disappeared. The possibilities were far and wide: maybe he had no internet connection or was busy with work or other things; maybe he was tired of exchanging emails with a stranger; maybe he had gone on a trip or was sick or had found a girlfriend who didn't like our conversations. Either way, I realized how much I missed his words. My desire to paint now seemed as far away as any impossible dream.

Then my thoughts went to John. We had shared the most intimate moment imaginable, but part of our connection had broken a little that weekend. And, denying all my instincts, I chose to ignore that fact, because he made me feel like I'd never felt before. After all, the things I'd discovered weren't all bad. He wasn't artistically or socially sensitive, but that was it. I convinced myself these problems were so minor that they would soon become insignificant in our relationship. Yes, I already thought of the two of us as being in a relationship, even if the thing couldn't be labeled (yet) as officially dating.

As my head traveled through the fog of uncertainty and assumptions, I was startled by a new email notification on my cell phone. Looking at the screen, my heart raced. It was Dark Angel. All doubts dissipated when I opened his message and began to read the words that I cherished so much.

"Black Rose,
First of all, I'm sorry about my absence. I had a very busy weekend and ended up with no time to respond to your email. I hope you haven't forgotten about me. I certainly haven't forgotten about you. Quite the contrary: these last few days, all I did was think about you. On Saturday, I visited my first art gallery. It was an amazing experience! I barely

knew where to look, where to start. But the person who was working there helped me out, and guess what? I bought a painting! I'm sending you a photo of it attached. I want to know what you think, but I'm very happy with the purchase.

Today I went shopping and got out of my comfort zone. I bought some clothes that I would have never even tried on before. I confess that I don't know if they will actually come out of the closet, but I will make an effort to wear them. I even bought a pair of colored pants, which I've never worn in my entire life (you must think I'm the most boring person on Earth right now, right?).

Anyway, that was my weekend. I hope you had as much fun as I did.

Responding to your last email, I think you're being too pessimistic. I firmly believe that when we get rid of something, especially a more-or-less job, it's because there's something better and bigger about to happen. Have faith.

I really liked your painting. And I honestly believe it does belong in a gallery like the one I visited. I didn't see anything there that your work doesn't have. The quality of your art is priceless, but more than that, you can see passion and dedication in every work you produce. It's a shame that, for one reason or another, you have to use the internet to get some exposure. However, I do believe you will do great things. I can't wait for it, as you certainly deserve it.

Well, it's late and I need to sleep, but I didn't want you to think that I forgot about you, so I decided to answer you before sleep caught me. Hope your week is amazing!

Xoxo,

Dark Angel"

After finishing reading, I felt a lightness of spirit. My ego savored his words voraciously, and a tremendous relief took over my being. Not only had he not forgotten about me, but he had also thought of me and done things due to my influence. I opened the image attached to the email and saw the picture of the painting he had bought. It was already hanging on the wall. The painting represented a lake surrounded by a forest that looked like something out of a fairy tale. It was truly very beautiful. I answered him promptly, still unable to contain my emotions much.

"Dark Angel,

What a joy to receive your message at the end of the day! I wondered if you had given up on our virtual friendship. I guess I can call it friendship, right? But I'm glad to hear that we'll continue our conversations.

What an exciting weekend! I think the painting you bought is beautiful. I am very grateful to have encouraged you to consume art. I also think it's great that you're out of your comfort zone when it comes to your wardrobe. I hope the experiments continue.

My weekend was good with its ups and downs. And as far as being pessimistic, I think you might have a point. But I try not to have too many expectations about life in general so as not to be disappointed. In any case, I hope you're right anyway, and that there's something better to come.

Thank you, once again, for your appreciation. I was quite unwilling to paint again, but your words gave me the spark I needed to think about continuing to produce. Maybe one day I'll also be in a gallery, right? (I'm not helping myself much with the no-expectations thing now).

I hope your week is great and that we talk more soon.

Xoxo,
Black Rose"

I lay down on the bed, experiencing the cozy, soft sensation of knowing my friend was still there for me. The uncertainties and hesitations I sometimes had about my own artwork disappeared after his validation. It was dangerous ground I was treading. I knew that clearly. But awareness of the thing didn't help control the emotions that danced through me, taking me in all directions with their random-step waltz.

I soon fell asleep, not realizing that the torpor was coming, although I woke up a few times during the night, which was something quite rare for me. I had nightmares but couldn't remember anything that had passed through my subconscious afterwards. I woke up before the alarm went off and tried to go back to sleep without success. So I stayed in bed for a while on my phone, checked social media and my email, then finally decided to get up. The house was quiet, and the noises of the city, our silence, were the only thing that could be heard. I went to the kitchen, made myself some coffee, and turned my attention, once again, to my cell phone. I filled the time with nonsense posted by my friends, irrelevant news about irrelevant people, and occasional important things about the world.

When it was time to go to college, I went to get ready. After the weekend full of revelations about John, however, my excitement to see him in class wasn't what it used to be. When he inhabited the world of ideas where I could mold him to my liking, the excitement to find the target of my fantasies was so intense that I could barely breathe. Now, something had changed. I still wanted to see him, of course, with an equally strong urge, but the part where I traveled in daydreams thinking about a future more present than any reality was gone.

The journey to college was more of the same. The city followed its daily course with a little pinch of depression because it was Monday. Tired faces, unrestrained yawns, and a characteristic bad mood of the mornings of the proletariat. The subway was packed, forcing me to stand for the entire ride. When I arrived at my destination, the energy of monotonous dissatisfaction had caught up with me. I felt the collective exhaustion weighing on my shoulders. It was still a little early. Class wouldn't start for at least fifteen minutes. I sat down on a bench a little farther away under a tree and busied myself, once again, with the uselessness that inhabited the applications on my cell phone. This time, in order to think even less, I played silly games to pass the time. When I realized I was almost late for class.

U pon arriving in the classroom, I sat on the first seat I saw unoccupied, and before I could settle in, the teacher arrived, just seconds after me. As he set his things on the desk himself, I looked around quickly and saw John sitting several rows in front of me. He hadn't seen me yet. At the sight of him, even from the back, my heart instantly sped up, and the world was suddenly more colorful. My worries about him became unimportant.

The teacher started the class quickly, and I turned my attention to him, even though my body stuck to its manifesto for feeling the presence of the man who moved me so much... so close. Every once in a while, I found myself turning my gaze back to where he was. We were halfway into the class, and he still hadn't noticed me. His focus seemed to be one hundred percent on what the professor was saying. Did I feel certain... resentment? No, no, it was another word, which perhaps did not yet exist in the vocabulary of the languages I knew, but I felt like that until the end of the class. Finally, just after the teacher had left, John turned around and saw me. When he noticed I was there, he smiled discreetly and walked over to me.

"Hey, I thought you weren't coming to class today. You're always early," he said as he leaned against my desk, toward me. His scent (of soap and aftershave) intoxicated me a little.

"I actually arrived early, but ended up losing track of time and only got inside when class was about to start."

"How did you sleep?"

"Well, well... and you?"

"Fine, too! Do you have time for coffee after class?"

I remembered that I had a job interview for that nanny position, but that wouldn't be until the afternoon. So I replied, "Yes, I do."

He smiled, and before he could respond, the teacher for the next class had arrived. John then returned to his desk. The rest of the school day passed quickly and I managed to keep my focus between the occasional jump of my core. At the end of the last class, John came back to me, already with his things in hand, and we walked to the coffee place where we had gone for our first "date." We talked about mundane things on the way. As usual, everything he said, no matter how banal, reached my ears with unnatural importance. I myself didn't have much to say, but I liked to hear him talk.

Upon arriving at the coffee house, I felt the immediate comfort of that cozy place. I ordered a black coffee, and he ended up having the same, although he added cream to his cup as soon as the waitress brought our orders. We took a few sips of our drinks, and John continued to fill the silence with everyday trifles. At one point, I remembered Kat's birthday party and invited him to come, not without some fear that he'd think it was a little too much for our very recent... relationship.

"I'd love to, of course," he replied with unexpected excitement.

Pleased with his reaction, I continued, "It will be on Friday. Just a few friends, nothing much. We plan to start at eight."

"Sounds great, I'll be there."

We went back to talking about trivial matters for a while longer, and then he said he had to go to work. He would take a cab, but first, he walked me to the subway, where we said goodbye with a quick kiss on the lips. It was amazing how the slightest contact with that man made my knees weak. I got on the train, still dealing with the shivers down my spine that his touch gave me. All the way home, I fantasized about having him once more in my intimate moments, with thoughts between imaginative conceptions and the real experiences we'd had together this past weekend.

When I got home, I realized I didn't have much more time to daydream about John. I needed to get ready for the job interview. So I changed quickly, took the letter of recommendation from my old boss, the mother of the children I'd taken care of for a while before I started working only at the diner, and headed back to the subway—the den of the hustle and bustle of modernity. In fact, haste was so devoted to the occasion that I didn't even have time to realize if I was nervous. The place was not far from the station I got off at, but I had to use my phone map to guide me, as I didn't know that neighborhood. After a few detours and getting lost along the way, I finally arrived at the family's home where I would potentially work.

I was received by a smiling young mother who was holding her baby in her arms. The girl was one-and-a-half years old, and as often happened to me when faced with the inherent sweetness of children, the affection was immediate. There were also two dogs in the house, who welcomed me warmly, wagging their tails excitedly and licking my hands as I bent down to pet them. We sat on the couch for the interview, and between questions and answers, the little girl already presented me with her approval, laughing at my funny faces, snuggling into my lap as if we were old friends. The conversation itself was smooth. I found out that the mother worked part-time in the afternoon, which was perfect for me, who went to school in the morning. I talked about my experiences and all. We discussed the payment, which in the US is usually set by the hour and paid once a week, and at the end, she basically said I was hired. I was happy with a feeling that I was on the right path. There was a friendly aura in the house. I would start the following week.

I left very satisfied with my life balance: new job, John and Dark Angel—mine. I wanted to go home and paint. On the way back, I took the opportunity to observe people and things and get inspired, focusing that feeling of happiness in the now. With the prospect of getting paid again, I decided that I would invest more in my art. I would buy more painting supplies, and in time when I was able to live alone, I would transform a room into an art studio. I let my imagination sail into the dangerous waters of fantasy once more that day. I visualized my little art studio with paintings everywhere and involuntary brushstrokes on the walls—mistakes that would turn into décor, raw, fresh!—in an atmosphere of my own, isolated from the rest of the world, where I could fully connect with art.

When I got home, the inspiring force that took me earlier lost an uphill battle to laziness—the mild sin was fading me away while my body melted into the abyss of the sofa. I read a little and then wandered between the TV and my phone, entertaining myself with nothings. Kat came home at night, bringing pizza and a case of beer. We ate and drank while I told her about my new job and she told me a little about her day. At one point, I remembered telling her that I had invited John to her birthday celebration. She was thrilled.

"I'm finally going to meet the mystery guy who's making you fall in love!"

I laughed but didn't deny her words this time. Kat was right, I knew it, and I decided to admit it there, to the silence of myself. John... he left me in a state of absolute, irrefutable rapture, as much as such a scenario unsettled me with its uncertainties. And, to be honest with myself, with every passing moment, I became more and more convinced that he felt the same way about me. Or something similar, at least. And this growing certainty made me immerse myself in the dreaded vulnerability. More and more.

That night, I couldn't fall asleep right away. I was excited about my new job and everything else going on around me, and the charge of vivacity filled my being. I thought about reading a little but

171

couldn't make up my mind to get out of bed. Once again, as modernity lets us, I decided to just stay on my cell phone—much easier than venturing into words that could make me fall into the clutches of thinking. The phone, of course, wouldn't help me fall asleep, but at least I wouldn't be alone with my thoughts. I looked at the clock—twenty past midnight. I had gone to bed before eleven o'clock. Before logging on to social media, I quickly checked my email. Between offers, promotions, and newsletters, there was a message from my dark angel. He had just sent it. I opened it and began to read, feeling, as always, the caress of his sweet words.

"Black Rose,
We can certainly call our relationship friendship. Although I don't even know your real name, I feel like I know you more than some of my long-time friends I see often. Of course, there is no justice in this comparison. After all, none of them can so masterfully translate the deepest human feelings through any art whatsoever. Anyway, I don't intend to give up on our conversations anytime soon! I hope the feeling is mutual.

I also really liked the painting. Now every time I look at it on my living room wall, I think of you.

As for the clothes, well, I haven't taken the tags off any of them yet, but one thing at a time. One day, who knows, I'll get to the point of wearing them in public. And without a doubt, I will continue with these experiments, at least with small things. It's very interesting to make choices that I wouldn't even have come close to considering before.

I totally understand this fear of creating expectations. It's a way of living, no doubt about it. But one must also give them (expectations) their due value. After all, it's what keeps us going, right? Dreams, goals, what would they be without expectations of success, you know? Of course, raising them too much can end in disappointment and suffering, but these also serve to teach us something. Anyway, choices...

I'm sure one day I'll see your work out there in an art gallery. So, don't stop creating, even if the will is almost nonexistent. It would be an inestimable loss to the rest of the world. Yes, I know it's selfish of me. I hope you'll forgive me. Your art doesn't belong to you alone, and it's not fair that people don't see it.

Xoxo,
Dark Angel"

Without thinking too much, just enjoying the fresh sensations, I hit the reply button on the email.

"Dark Angel,

*Undoubtedly, the feeling of friendship is recipro-
cal. Having these conversations with you makes me
very happy. I think, in a way, we know each other
better than anyone else. It turns out to be easy to let
certain vulnerabilities out when there's no fear of
judgment. In a strange way, I trust you more for this
than a friend who knows my face, my name, and my
story.*

*Well, tell me about your little experiments, please.
I myself may also start to step out of my comfort
zone a little. It's never easy, but it can bring some
very pleasant surprises.*

*Regarding expectations, once again, you are
right. It's dangerous to get carried away by them,
but I suppose without that sense of purpose to
achieve, we wouldn't do half of the things we should
be doing. In any case, as romantic as the idea
that suffering is good is (which I admit it's true),
it doesn't mean that we necessarily want to go
through it (I know I don't).*

*I don't know if one day I'll be in an art gallery.
After all, it's not just talent that counts for these
things. In fact, there are more mediocre talents occupying successful spaces than you'd think. But I
hope one day I can achieve something. For now, I'll*

do what I can. By the way, speaking of doing what I can, I got another job. It's not a dream job yet, but I feel like it's going to be better than what I was doing before. That's something, right?

Sometimes (most of the time) I think you see too much in me. I won't stop making art, but to say the world would lose something is a bit much. Don't think I'm displaying false modesty or that I'm looking for compliments from you, it's just how I really feel. I recognize and enjoy my own work, but I know the world would be fine without it, as there are countless wonderful artists who grace us with their art.

I hope your week is going well.
Xoxo,
Black Rose"

After replying to my friend's email, I was suddenly overcome with sleepiness. The lightness of my feelings had led me to close my eyes and lulled me into sweet dreams of which my consciousness wanted to make a home. This being an impossible wish, it was with frustration that I woke up the next day to the violent sound of the alarm on my phone.

T hat day went on like so many other days that end up forgotten somewhere in the back of the mind—nothing but the uneventful monotony. In fact, it was like that for the rest of that week. On school days, I spent quite a bit of time with John. When he didn't have to go straight to work after college, we'd have coffee together. Besides that, nothing. Dark Angel still hadn't responded to my email, but I no longer worried with uncertainty. I knew now that he certainly hadn't forgotten about me, and no doubt his absence was due to lack of time or something of the sort.

Friday arrived after the days had dragged on for an eternity of boredom. Finally, some excitement was rising in my being with Kat's party happening that night. I was thrilled at the prospect of introducing John to my friend and having him with me outside of school hours. Besides, if I would be completely honest with myself, I was a little proud of being able to show him off in that social circle. His extreme handsomeness, so standard, so expected, the fact that he chose to be with me fed my thirsty ego.

That day, after class and coffee with John, I went straight home. The enthusiasm of getting everything ready for the night took me by the hands. Kat had bought snacks and filled the fridge with beers, as well as bottles and bottles of every kind of liquor you can think of. We would order pizza—no *carne louca* and *coxinhas*, typical party foods from Brazil—and I was responsible for making *caipirinhas*. While she was still working, I tidied up the apartment and rearranged the furniture to make more room for the guests. Although she said she wouldn't invite many people, my roommate was extremely popular, and besides, her friends also had friends who had friends who had friends...

After putting everything in order, I connected a pair of Kat's small speakers to my computer and put together some playlists with upbeat songs that were playing on the radio lately. I could already visualize the delight of the hypnotic dance that the poetry of catchy phrases and repetitive harmony would bring; a collective enjoyment, music. I also had napkins, plates, and disposable cups on the table where the food and drinks would be. And I enjoyed, for a second, the delight of having everything organized. At almost the same moment, she arrived home, thanked me for taking care of the tidying up, and then we started getting ready. With the beautification of the house finished, the irrefutable second step, obviously, would be to adorn ourselves as well.

It didn't take long for people to start arriving. Gradually, the apartment was filled with the sounds of random conversations, which, with time and alcohol, became more and more enthusiastic. Kat introduced me to everyone who came in, and some people had to be introduced to her too—friends of friends of friends. And she insisted on telling all the guests that I was Brazilian. And I smiled uneasily at each comment that followed the information: do you like soccer; what a coincidence, my cousin's girlfriend is from South America; ah, carnaval, huh; etc., etc., etc. I was almost used to it. But, in the depths of my thoughts, the thing was still problematized. The birthday girl also insisted that all the guests tried the *caipirinha*—too strong for some, but most people liked the *exotic* cocktail.

Time passed, and although I myself was starting to enjoy the excitement with which all the drinking presented me, I began to feel a little apprehensive that John still hadn't arrived—not even texted. I thought about asking him, texting him myself, but I didn't want the humiliation of not seeming carefree. So, in order to push the anxiety into the locked box at the back of my mind, I engaged in conversation and food and drinks and music. At the end of a few minutes (or was it seconds? hours?), I no longer thought about John.

Despite the nice atmosphere, the party was nowhere near the ones we have in Brazil. There was a—mild—atmosphere of fun. The more upbeat songs played, but no one moved. I missed the barbecue parties and everyone dancing the millimetrically choreographed 1990s *axé* songs and the parties with *coxinha*, *bolinho de queijo*, and *brigadeiro* from my homeland. *Well, at least the beer here was better*, I consoled myself. As I thought about it, there was a knock on the door. When I got up and walked over to it, I found myself staggering a little. Maybe I should hold off on the alcohol, a voice in the background of my thoughts whispered. I opened the door, saw John. He looked gorgeous, as usual, in his customary style: jeans, white T-shirt, and leather jacket. He held a case of beer in his hand—my favorite beer. We smiled at each other, and I invited him in.

"You look beautiful," he said.

"You, too. Thanks for the beer."

He followed me into the kitchen, and I put the beer in the fridge. Then I took his jacket to place it in my room—all while my heartbeat sped almost to the point I felt it ripping through my chest, breaking the fragile skin in a bizarre, passionate dance. On the way, we bumped into Kat, who was all smiles and just as drunk as I was, or even more, probably more. She looked at us expectantly and I made the appropriate introductions.

"John, this is Kat, my roommate, and the birthday girl. Kat, this is John."

He hurried to extend his hand to her, but my friend decided to hug him instead of the typical cold handshake. He looked a little startled, but reciprocated, saying, "Nice to meet you, and happy birthday!"

"Thanks, the pleasure is all mine," Kat replied, and you could tell from her voice that the spirits of drunkenness took over her. Holding on to his arm, she continued, "I've heard so much about you. I can't believe we finally met. Clara, she... you are so lucky to have this amazing woman."

He smiled and answered, "I completely agree."

Someone called Kat's name, and she, without excusing herself, disappeared among the small mass of people. We went to my bedroom, and inside, after throwing his jacket on the bed, I turned to John.

"Sorry for Kat's attitude, but you know how it is. She's been drinking since so early. We have been."

He laughed casually. "You don't need to apologize. It's her birthday. Today is Friday and a day to celebrate."

As he spoke, on an unrestrained impulse, I got closer to him and wrapped my arms around his shoulders. A kind of dizzy heat was who I was, there, in that now. I looked into his eyes intensely, kissed him on the lips; first softly and then harder, almost violently. I don't know how much time passed, but we stood there exchanging caresses and caresses—our bodies seemed linked by magnetism, that cliché so real in that instant—until we were interrupted by someone opening the door. Scare, guilt?... It was a friend of Kat's who was looking for the bathroom. After pointing to the right door, we ended up also leaving to join the rest of the party—another form of contentment.

"What do you want to drink?" I asked John. "I made *caipirinhas* if you're interested."

He promptly replied, "Um, I want to try it."

So I took the drink, which was in a pitcher, and poured it into a plastic cup, adding some ice. He took a sip and made an approving expression. "Very good."

Although I was already a little drunk, I poured myself a glass, too, and we sat there, chatting about unimportant pleasantries while we drank. Our conversations were never very deep, but I quite enjoyed talking to him anyway. I liked his voice and intonation, the way he pronounced the words, and also the gestures that followed them. The content of the conversation became almost irrelevant when we were together since the senses commanded me in those moments.

The notion of time, and even of space, became lost as the night went on. John and I laughed a lot and occasionally engaged in casual conversation with whoever was around. The glasses were filling and emptying, and the songs continued to play, one after the other. Some people were kissing on the couch while others were busy with their drinks or smoking on the porch. A guy had passed out in an armchair. A voice in the back of my mind whispered that we should turn the volume down, but the party noise drowned out its murmur. I don't know how one of the neighbors didn't decide to call the police, for although I had no idea what time it was, I was pretty sure it was past midnight—at least.

At some point, however, the guests began to leave. There were now about ten people in the house when we heard a knock on the door. Surely some complaining neighbor. Kat and I went to answer it together, and when we opened the door, we found Jordan, her ex. For a few seconds, the three of us just stood there, not saying a word. The shock brought me certain instant sobriety. I looked at the time on the DVD player's dial: one-forty in the morning. Then my eyes went to John who, sensing something was happening, walked over to us and stood beside me. Finally, Kat spoke up.

"Jordan?! What the hell are you doing here at this hour?" She also seemed to have sobered up abruptly.

"Kat, how come you didn't invite me to your birthday party?" His tearful, altered voice indicated that he too had been drinking that night.

My friend responded with an expression that mixed indignation and genuine anger. Her eyes blazed with such vigor that I was afraid she would physically attack him. Instead, she just said "Good night, Jordan."

And she started to close the door, but he stopped her, holding it with his hand as he came inside. By this time, someone had turned off the music, and everyone was paying attention to what was happening. John intervened, placing himself between Kat and Jordan.

"Hey, bro, she said 'good night.' I think you should go."

Jordan confusedly looked at him and, for a moment, seemed to think about what to do next. I held my breath, fearing the situation would escalate, the toxic masculinity mixed with the alcohol that took over the surroundings making a point of showing itself alive. Finally, my friend's ex replied.

"Look, I don't know who you are, but I just came to wish my girlfriend a happy birthday."

"I'm not your girlfriend, Jordan!" Kat stated angrily.

Jordan then turned to her again and, to everyone's amazement, began to cry like a child. For several seconds, only the sound of his wailing was heard in the apartment. My friend was looking at him desperately now, probably like the rest of us, not knowing what to do.

"I love you, Kat," he began to say through sobs. "You broke my heart when you broke up with me."

"You're moving away," she replied, her voice a little softer now, but still filled with resentment. "You chose to leave me."

He sobbed again while shaking his head.

"I know, I know, it's my fault..."

The silence broken by his laments returned. Once again, John, who was watching the scene closely, decided to intervene. He approached Jordan and, giving him a friendly pat on the shoulder, said, "I know how you feel. But it's very late. Everyone is aggravated. Go home now, take a shower, go to sleep, and tomorrow, who knows, you can talk about it if you both want to. Okay?"

Jordan looked at him with a mixture of doubt and gratitude. Finally, he agreed. "Alright, alright. Kat, I'm sorry I showed up unannounced."

She just stared at him silently.

"I'll get a car on my phone," I said, as I took out my cell phone.

John then went downstairs with Jordan to wait. They were followed by the rest of the people who were still there—uncomfortable goodbyes: *you know, it's late, but happy birthday again, bye.* There's nothing like an awkward moment to disperse those only looking for Friday night entertainment.

We were now alone in the apartment. I sat with Kat on the couch to try to comfort her—an arduous task when you're afraid of other people's pain and you don't really have the gift of gab on your side.

"How are you?" I asked, although the answer to that question was already crystal clear.

"I don't know," she replied, "a mixture of anger and sadness. I really didn't expect him to show up here, especially in the middle of the night and on my birthday. What's wrong with guys?"

"Yeah, I don't know. But he was drunk. Tomorrow he will for sure be sorry and apologize to you."

"I don't even want him to do that. I don't want to hear from him ever again!"

Her eyes changed all the time, transitioning between anger and pain. Such bitterness was not unknown to me—nor to all women who date men, probably. There was no solace for her but time. But, as friendship presumes, I tried anyway.

"You know, you're going to find someone a lot better than him, and when that day comes, you'll thank heavens you got rid of this guy."

"Yeah, I know," she said with resignation, "but in the meantime, the pain will go on for a while."

How to extract a word of comfort from the truth? I couldn't think of anything to say, so I hugged her instead. We lay there, half-lying on the sofa, not speaking, just absorbed in the moment of that sisterly sharing. After a while, I noticed that she had fallen asleep, her head on my shoulder. I got up, took off her shoes, and covered her with a blanket. At that moment, I heard the sound of the door opening. It was John returning.

"Well, he's gone," he said, and, looking at Kat, continued, "I'm glad she fell asleep."

"Yes, she needs to rest," I replied, "thanks for taking care of the situation."

"Don't worry about it. I didn't want to impose, but at the same time I realized that you guys were a little lost."

"Quite lost."

"What's their story anyway? As we waited for the car, he just cried and told me he loved her."

"Ugh!" I rolled my eyes indignantly. "Well, basically, they used to go out, but they never officially dated. So not long ago he said he was moving to California, and she broke up with him."

"I see," John replied, showing no particular emotion. "That sucks."

I just nodded. I wondered what his real opinion on the matter was, if any, but my energy was drained, so instead of asking him, or asking *myself,* I preferred to close the thing inside my head. I was getting good at locking up uncomfortable reflections under lock and key.

"Well," I said casually, "do you want to go to bed?"

In fact, I wasn't even sure he would stay over. I just assumed he would. The assumption made me think, right after I asked him that question, that it might seem like an imposition. But he just replied, "Yes, yes. It's been a long night."

☞⟩⟩⟩ ⟨⟨⟨☜

L ying there, open eyes staring at the ceiling, I realized that despite the extreme feeling of mental fatigue, sleep was not going to come easily. John was already fast asleep, light breathing, heavy body. A few minutes ago, we looked like a single human being, possessing two bodies that fit together perfectly. The harmony found in sex, that night fast and unrestrained, was so rhythmic and heavenly that it was impossible for me not to think of this man as some kind of soul mate if there was such a thing. With him, I felt ethereal, spiritual, and comfortable, like I could relax until there were no more shadows, no more fears.

However, now that the orgasms had passed, I found myself awake, crammed into my single bed with him, not knowing what to do with my body to make it a little more comfortable. After a few moments of trying to give myself any kind of rest, I ended up succumbing to the stimulus that wouldn't let me sleep. So I decided to look at my phone until my mind would finally hear my exhausted body screaming and calling for a truce. What was my surprise when, in this unassuming act, I came across an email from Dark Angel. My heart smiled—a smile that reached my lips too, shy, sly...guilty? I began to read.

"Black Rose,
I'm glad you consider me your friend. Our conversations make me happy too, and I think you're

right in the conclusion that it turns out to be easier to trust each other than people in the 'real world.'

Sorry for the delay in writing you back, but you know how work is, always getting in the way of important things. I'll try not to let that happen too much.

About my experimentation, well, let's see: I'm trying new restaurants, giving music I'd never heard before a chance, and most recently, I've tried a new wine. I know it doesn't sound like much, but for me, it's a significant change (I've been drinking the same wines for years). Pathetic, I know... but don't give up on me, please!

I'm so glad you found a new job. This is great! It may not be your dream job, but it is definitely a step in the right direction. And that's how, little by little, you must learn to moderate the expectations we talked about and, of course, finally come to live out of your art.

I never thought you were someone who seeks praise masked as modesty. I know you don't see yourself with my eyes. And those eyes, they don't see 'too much' in you, Black Rose. I know there is a plethora of amazing artists out there, but what you need to understand is that I place you among them.

Have a great weekend.

Xoxo,

Dark Angel"

I answered him right away. It was a little weird doing it with John sleeping next to me—an enigmatic sense of transgression. Not that I thought of Dark Angel in a romantic way (at least that's what I told myself), but it was still impossible for me to conceive of a world in which the two of them coexisted.

"Dark Angel,
Undoubtedly, it ends up being easier to trust someone whose name or face is not known, but only their thoughts about so many important things, such as art. And no need to apologize for taking too long to respond. I know how crazy life can sometimes be, full of responsibilities.
I think the changes you've been experiencing are actually a lot. After all, how many of us can say we venture into new seas, no matter how small?
I'm indeed excited about the new job, to be honest. It sure is something. I hope that one day I can, if not make a living out of my art, at least earn some extra money and have a little recognition.
Well, I already have your admiration, don't I? Maybe one day I'll touch some art critic or gallery

owner or something like that the same way I touched you?

Have a great weekend too!
Xoxo,
Black Rose"

After sending the email, I just lay there, enjoying the sweet sensation that my virtual friend's words always brought me, and which endured. Without realizing it, the comfort in my heart manifested itself in my body at last, which, now cozy, suddenly ended up falling asleep.

I found myself in a strangely familiar place. Some part of me knew I was inside of a dream. That part wondered if I'd ever dreamed of this before. It was a living room—no, a kind of library or office. Infinite shelves filled with books of different languages, some armchairs next to a lit fireplace, and a big desk in the corner. Sitting at the desk, a man was leafing through some papers that, by his worried expression, must have been documents of the utmost importance. The man looked like something out of an old movie. He wore a suit and tie, a hat, and sported a prominent mustache. Upon noticing my presence in the room, he looked at me with what appeared to be pitying eyes.

"So, Clara," the man began to say, and his voice was grave and austere, "you've been communicating with him, haven't you?"

Not understanding, I looked at him with a doubtful expression. He seemed to expect a more concrete answer from me, so I replied, "I don't know what you're talking about. With who?"

He returned his gaze to his documents and, with a wave of his hands, ordered me to come closer. When I was beside him, he pointed to one of the sheets of paper and, looking at it, for some reason, I couldn't read it. However, even without the ability to decipher those signs, I understood that they were the emails I exchanged with Dark Angel. I then turned to the man.

"How did you get those emails?"

He looked at me as if I was a naive child who doesn't know the least about life and replied, "I have the power to get whatever I want."

His eyes then turned into flames. I got scared and tried to back away, but he caught me by the arms.

"You did something very wrong, Clara."

In tears, unable to contain the gigantic fear that seized me when I saw that man face-to-face, I replied, "But what's wrong with exchanging emails with someone?"

He looked even more furious, and his voice turned into something dark as he replied. "You know about your own wrongdoing."

Still holding my arms, he got closer to me. I could feel, more and more, the heat of the fire in his eyes burning, stinging, igniting... when his face almost touched mine, I abruptly woke up, my whole body bathed in sweat.

John was no longer beside me, but the noise I heard from outside indicated that he was around. Sweat was still running down my forehead and sticking the bedding to my naked body. My heart throbbed. I shook my head, shook off the night-mare, got up, took quick steps to the bath-room—washed face, washed soul. I put on an old T-shirt and shorts and headed to the kitchen, where the sounds of life came from. When I got there, I saw John preparing some eggs. Kat was also present, sitting, sipping on a cup of coffee. The two looked comfortable, chatting about the day before.

"Good morning," I said and they both turned to me.

"Good morning," Kat replied. "John made coffee and insisted on cooking breakfast."

I went to him, kissed him on the cheek. He smiled.

"Good morning. Did you sleep well?" he asked after kissing my forehead.

"Like a baby," I lied. "And you?"

"Same. I ended up blacking out really fast. I was exhausted."

Turning now to Kat, I asked, "How are you?"

"Oh, I'm fine, I guess. You know, it's not easy, but we have to move on."

"Any news from Jordan?"

"No. And I hope he leaves me alone."

After that, silence. For long seconds, all you could hear was the noise of John handling ingredients and utensils. The clink of the spatula in the pan, the hiss of the food meeting the bubbling butter, even the sound of smoke forming seemed to exist inside the kitchen, maybe even echoing through the rest of the apartment, and beyond. At one point, he announced that the meal was ready. All at the table; he served scrambled eggs, toast, and bacon. I was starving. My body often cried out for nourishment and comfort after a night of drinking. We ate while talking about unimportant things. They ended up getting into an argument about football and, in my ignorance of the subject, I took the opportunity to be alone with my thoughts while just nodding my head now and then as if I was a little there—but I wasn't.

I thought about my nightmare. Did I feel that much guilt for having a relationship, however platonic, with Dark Angel while dating John? It didn't make sense, but maybe my subconscious didn't care about logic. In any case, I would not give up either of these men in my life, and the decision, set in stone within me, satisfied me as heresy satisfies the sinner. John completed me physically and emotionally and my dark angel, artistically and intellectually. If they were one person, I'm pretty sure I'd start to believe in soulmates. I think this junction would make a complete and perfect human being. So, without realizing it, I lost myself in these pointless daydreams for I don't know how long. Until I heard my name and realized that the real world demanded my attention.

"Clara?" Kat was saying insistently.

"Yea?" I replied, turning to her.

"Where have you been?"

"Um... I just got distracted for a moment. You know football is not my thing."

"But that subject was over. We were talking about summer break. I told John that your plans are to 'work on your thesis.'" That last line was said with as much disapproval as possible.

"Well...yes," I replied simply, then took a sip of coffee.

Kat rolled her eyes disapprovingly.

John chuckled and said, "I was just telling her that I plan to use a few days to visit my family. You know, eating home-cooked meals, taking a little road trip..."

"Oh, that's great," I replied, smiling.

"I was wondering," he continued, "if maybe you'd like to go with me."

Surprised. Flattered. My heart, before resting in serenity, seemed to have, at the same time, stopped beating and began a symphony of accelerated notes. I replied immediately. "Sure, I would love to."

And in that instant, in my mind, John was back to being the only man who made sense. The only possible man. At least for a moment, which was, after all, what mattered—that present moment. When summer comes, the warmth of the sun will witness our connection expand and rise, my inner voices told me. And my heart, body, mind, and soul were already throbbing with anxiety.

Summer

B orn and raised in a tropical country, I imagined that the American summer would gently embrace me and that I would laugh at its attempt to warm up the surroundings. After all, in
São Paulo, temperatures border this season almost
all year round. However, there was something uncomfortable about the heat of the United States,
at least in the part of the country where I was at.
I can't quite describe what. The climate seems to
be wetter, denser, an almost palpable burning sensation. Luckily, there was air conditioning everywhere (heaven forbid Americans from experiencing any kind of discomfort). The finite space of that
rental car, therefore, was more than bearable. In
fact, I felt extremely comfortable.

John was an excellent driver and wore a smile that
went well with the sunglasses he had on. The radio
was turned on to a station that played trendy music,
usually pop and hip-hop. In the trunk, two wheeled

suitcases and a backpack contained the essentials for a weekend in suburban New York. It took me a while to get used to the definition of a suburb here: smaller cities, the so-called towns, commonly inhabited by people of the middle or upper classes. My head was still confused between sign and meaning and the word, when pronounced, always took me to Brazil and the clusters of people on the hills, the beat-up cars with loud music, the illegal trade in the streets, the people and their pain.

I was wrapped in a mixture of anxiety and excitement. Anxiety (with all the negative charge of the word) because I would meet his family—and you never really know what to expect from such a meeting. Ah, the countless possibilities! But deep down, I had a credulous hope that they would be nice—my only reason being John. His family of origin couldn't be so out of touch with his own personality. Could it? In any case, there was also the exciting part of the thing. If John was taking me on a trip to meet his parents, our relationship was undoubtedly reaching new levels. He hadn't asked me to be his girlfriend, but we'd been dating for a good few months now. We saw each other every day there was class and almost every weekend. He spent a lot of time at my place. I also went to his apartment from time to time, but I preferred the other way around—his place was always a mess, and it was hard to make sense there.

As I thought about these things and dealt with conflicting emotions, I also paid attention to the journey. From my window, I could see that the landscape suddenly changed from very tall buildings, a lot of traffic, and concrete, to a world that, until then, was covered by the almost oblivion in me. I didn't remember in my day-to-day life that there were still places where nature predominated. Many, many trees, some still in bloom from spring, now graced our path. I was moved by the sight. It looked like postcards or pictures found in country house paintings. It looked unreal, almost fake, a movie set made out of cardboard and paper-mâché. A sudden inspiration took me. What a pity—I couldn't draw anything inside of a moving car. But I promised myself that I would hold on to the feeling.

"So what do you think?" John asked suddenly, snapping me out of my thoughts.

"The view is incredible!" I replied with excitement. "It's so green that I can't conceive that you people call my country a 'jungle.'"

He laughed heartily and so did I.

"Well, you have the Amazon, right?!"

"Yeah, yeah, I know. But for me, who comes from a big city, it's crazy to think about this vision that the world has of Brazil."

"I can imagine," he replied and added, after a short pause, "you're going to flip out when we get to my town, then. It's completely different from New York City. What kind of animals have you seen there so far?"

"Uh, mostly squirrels."

"Yeah, get ready to see a lot of those and more."

I looked at him with some... apprehension.

"Like what?"

"Oh, deer, raccoons... if we're lucky, maybe even a bear?"

My surprised expression must have been hilarious, as John laughed again, this time letting the laughter take over for a considerable amount of time.

"No need to be afraid," he said after he had collected himself. "We probably won't see any."

"Oh, well, that's comforting," I replied sarcastically.

For the next few moments, we got into a heated argument about living with wild animals, which was completely normal for him and extremely strange for me. In the end, we agreed that they had more rights than we did to occupy any space at all.

Finally, we arrived at our destination. He took the exit, and as we drove into town, feelings washed over me. The sensation was like the one I had when I first arrived in New York City—as if I was inside a movie or a dream or some parallel universe. The houses were beautiful with their lawns and white picket fences, which certainly served only as an adornment as most were no taller than a child. Some of the houses didn't even have that, which made me think of the iron gates and high concrete walls of São Paulo. Besides, we seldom saw any businesses. At first, what I saw were just these cute homes that looked more like they were made to be inhabited by dolls. However, when we arrived on the main street of the city, according to John, I saw some shops and restaurants. Everything around was very adorable, almost childlike, bringing a fairy-tale feeling.

After a few more minutes of driving around town, minutes in which I was absorbed in enchantment, we arrived at John's mother's house. His father lived in an apartment not far away, he told me as I thought about how absurd life is sometimes—me being there, at that apex, the dream man beside me and his childhood home in front of me. The house was, like all the others around, very large and beautiful. There was no fence around it, just the manicured lawn with bushes and colorful flowers. John parked on the concrete in front of the garage door. They called it *driveway*. For some reason, they didn't use their garages to store their cars (John told me that instead, they used them for hoarding).

We got out of the car, and John busied himself with getting our bags. And I kept observing. There was a path to the front door in the middle of the lawn made of red bricks in a very retro style. For its entire length, rocks so perfect they looked fake were arranged along the edges of the small path. As we reached the door, I noticed that there was one of those knocker things, which looked like it had been taken from an old castle. John, instead of knocking, rang the bell. *Okay, it's now* went through my head, the growing tension taking over. I was about to face the reality of what this person would be like. Until then, she existed only in what my imagination was capable of conceiving as a possibility.

We heard footsteps approaching a few moments after the shrill sound of the doorbell faded. The door then opened to a smiling woman who hugged her son affectionately. She was very pretty and exuded a youthful energy. She had blond hair, and her blue eyes were identical to John's. She wore a flowered dress, and her feet were bare. After the long welcome to him, she broke free and looked at me with sympathy and curiosity. But before we could be introduced, she gestured for us to enter the house.

As soon as we walked through the door, I came across a beautiful living room, the kind you find in decoration magazines or on social media. John put the bags aside and we both sat on the couch. His mother sat in the armchair across from us and he finally said, "Mom, this is Clara. Clara, my mother, Dorothy."

I got up and went to her for a moment, holding out my hand, which she shook firmly.

"Nice to meet you," I said with the best smile I could muster.

"The pleasure is all mine," she replied, also smiling.

I went back to my seat, and Dorothy asked if we wanted something to drink. We both asked for water and she went to the kitchen for a moment.

"Everything okay?" asked John in a whisper.

"Great," I replied.

He smiled with relief and satisfaction, and she returned carrying two glasses of water, which we drank while chatting. She asked me about my story and my likes and dislikes and my life. I told her briefly, without much detail, how I got there. I talked a little about my family in Brazil, my plans for the future, and about my impressions of the United States, emphasizing the stark difference between New York City and John's small and graceful hometown.

Dorothy listened to me attentively, shaking her head at times—polite, even friendly. The chat was permeated with trivialities and praise. She congratulated me on my courage in leaving my country and extolled my skills in the English language and insinuated that she thought I was beautiful. I praised her beautiful house and her manners and her beauty too. All very clumsy—on my part, of course. She seemed very diplomatic, carrying the conversation with a grace I could never achieve. Then she showed me the rest of the house. Each room captivated me more than the last and I felt that I was going through a tunnel that took me to a new world, previously unknown and as far away as the confines of knowledge as yet undiscovered. The decoration details, the extreme cleanliness, and tidiness evidenced how important her home was to that woman. When she showed us the room where we would be staying, we decided to stay there and take the opportunity to get some rest.

I lay down on the bed next to John, who almost immediately fell asleep. I, on the other hand, although I had woken up very early and suffered the weariness of exhausting emotions, could not fall asleep. The commotion of that day's events was fresh in my head, as if it was, in fact, still happening—and perhaps it was. I decided to keep part of it inside me—the nervousness, the overwhelming expectations, and the good pain of the intensity of things. The other part, I was determined to try to give life to—all the inspiration I'd had along the way. I got up from bed, then, looking for something that would serve me as a tool. I found a notebook and some pens in the drawer of one of the desks and sat down on the floor, opening the notebook and resting it on my bent legs as I began to draw.

My sketch started with a metropolitan landscape. Tall buildings, cars, and a sun that, hidden behind an edifice, was barely noticeable in the drawing. However, in the middle of the page, this view merged with the natural spectacle that was taken by flowering trees and full foliage. Birds occupied part of the sky and a rabbit could be seen in movement, running through the bushes. Simple shading, done with the same black pen used to draw; carefree traits; draft ready—drawing ready. I got up, then, and left the creation, the notebook, and the pen on a bedside table. Then, drained of everything, I spent a few minutes staring out the window, aimlessly. It overlooked the backyard of the house. There was a swimming pool, a vast lawn, a grill, and a table surrounded by chairs. It seemed like the perfect place to gather friends. For a tantalizing second, I imagined myself sitting there, a glass of wine in my hand, making small talk with these people as if I belonged. I chased away the thought, in fear of my own hope.

I was easily distracted, I realized right away, with this view and these perspectives that only existed in me. I "woke up" with the sound of a new notification on my cell phone. I looked at John, afraid he'd woken up with the noise, but he only turned a little to the side and then returned to the sleeping state he'd been in before. I almost envied him. I looked at my phone screen and saw an automated message from my bank in Brazil saying I was eligible for a loan or something like that—I didn't read anything other than the title. My finger went to the option to delete the email, and I sighed with forced but, nonetheless, aching resignation. I hadn't spoken to Dark Angel in a while—at least two weeks. And that was an immensity, since, lately, we exchanged messages almost every day.

Our communication, mine and Dark Angel's, gradually became more and more casual, and we started talking about things beyond philosophical issues from a social point of view and art. Now, mixed with the discussion of the elitization of artistic expressions, we talked about when his car had to be repaired or when I arrived almost an hour late for college because of a delay on the subway or when his dog got sick and he had to rush to the vet—and how alienation takes over social spaces and how difficult life is for new artists and all things that permeate the world of ideas, but also the concrete world, which we touch and feel, smell, taste...

On top of all that, I no longer felt guilty about messaging my friend. In fact, he was now as much a part of my life as anyone else—even John. He didn't know about Dark Angel, of course, but the relevance of the information to that part of my existence seemed nil now.

These reflections led me to nostalgia—a peculiar nostalgia, not for something that was in the past, so to speak, but a lack, a... I don't know. All I know is that this feeling, whatever it was, made me reread some of our conversations. I had created a special folder in my email for our messages and opened one of them—the craving for something, anything, from him.

"Black Rose,
How is this first week of work going? I hope it lives up to expectations. I don't know what you do,

really, but whatever it is, focus on the positives. Unless, of course, the negatives are intolerable. If so, it's not worth it.

Speaking of work, I'm starting a project with a new artist. I'm excited at the prospect. I haven't seen any of his work yet, but my boss said he's really good. Maybe I can get you some market insights?

By the way, any new paintings or drawings? I miss enjoying your art. I hope work is not an impediment for you to produce. It's a shame we have to give so much of our time to the task of making money, don't you think?

Anyway, tell me how things are going. Rooting for you.

Xoxo,
Dark Angel"

My reply to that email was there too, and I set about reading it also, to relive the conversation as a whole.

"Dark Angel,
It's true, I never told you what I do. Well, the previous job I had was as a waitress, and now I'm a nanny. I've done this before and while it's not my life goal, I quite enjoy it. My first week is going

great. For now, there are definitely no intolerable downsides to this job.

Wow, how interesting that you're going to work with an artist. I would love to get tips from him, no doubt. But, tell me, what do YOU do exactly?

I don't have any new art at the moment, but I don't want to let work, or anything else, be an obstacle for me to continue producing. In fact, as soon as I'm done writing this message, I'm going to work on something.

And yes, I think it's really sad that we have to dedicate most of our time to work. That's why it's so important to do something you like, in my opinion.

Hope all is well.

Xoxo,

Black Rose"

The next email had been answered almost immediately. Before reading it, I noticed that was the moment when our relationship had reached another level. From then on, a new range of understandings that we had about each other had opened up. Now we were no longer disembodied creatures that only existed in the created small cyber world. We were people with jobs, who got up early, made money, and were part of real life.

However, even though I had this knowledge, the subtle aspect of our relationship was still there. Dark Angel was indeed an individual who occupied a space in society, but for me, he was also this other being, almost celestial, as immaterial and impalpable as an angel but of an importance that only a person of faith in this creature would know how to describe.

With these thoughts crowding my mind, I continued reading.

"Black Rose,

Wow, you have the hardest job in the world, in my opinion. And one of the most important too. I'm glad that everything is going well at work and that you enjoy what you do. Very rare for that to happen these days. But, as we said, this is actually very important. After all, most of our hours are spent working.

I have a much more boring job: I'm a lawyer. This artist I'm working with needs help with image copyrights. Nothing too exciting, but every now and then I end up meeting interesting people and having experiences that make it worthwhile. Despite everything, I like my job. I'm not very good at many other things to choose to change, anyway.

Yay, I'm really looking forward to seeing what you'll produce next. It doesn't matter if it's just a draft, please send it to me. I miss appreciating your art, which is so unique and speaks to me so intensely.

Xoxo,
Dark Angel"

Before I could read the response I gave him, my attention went back to John, who was moving around in the bed. I thought he had woken up and I kept waiting for him to get up, but in vain. It was just a light sleep, perhaps even fraught with dreams, that made his body too energized to fall asleep completely. After a few moments of waiting, I got back to my emails.

"Dark Angel,
Yes, I believe that being responsible for children is really one of the hardest jobs there is. But for one reason or another, I've always had an easy time with the task. In fact, I prefer a thousand times to work with children than with adults. They are more outspoken and, frankly, understand things faster than grown-ups, most of the time.

Wow, lawyer... How important! I don't think it's a boring profession, at least from the point of view of my not-very-comprehensive knowledge on the subject. I don't think I would be able to do that, because, in addition to the obvious obstacles (the fact that I'm not good at convincing people of any-thing), I wouldn't be able to handle the mental load that must be attached to this kind of work. I admire you so much for being able to do that. And you said you're not good at other things, but I have to strongly disagree: you're very good with words!

I ended up scribbling something on a piece of paper I found on my desk, and since you want to see something so badly, I'm sending you a photo at-tached. Maybe I'll go back to work on this drawing and turn it into something real, I don't know.

Xoxo,

Black Rose"

I paused my reading once more, thinking about the steps we had taken on our journey together. My relationship with Dark Angel seemed to have reached an even higher level of intimacy than my relationship with John. It was funny to think that the guy I had sex with wasn't as close to me as the guy I just chatted with over the internet, but this was a truth—one of those absurd truths that, however, leaves no room for questioning or denial.

My eyes wandered back to our conversations. I skipped some emails, stopped in some sections for a longer time than the rest, went back to the ones from the early days... I played with the notion of present, past, and future, permeating through words that took me to those moments' particles. Although being a false sensation, it was good to feel like I was manipulating time.

⟫⟫⟫ ⟪⟪⟪

I was interrupted by a cough from John. He sat up, this time actually waking up. I closed my email app, went to him.

"How long ago did you wake up?" he asked, still half asleep.

"I couldn't sleep, actually," I replied as I sat beside him on the bed.

John stretched and then hugged me, pulling me to him. We lay there for a long time, not saying anything, just enjoying the torpor of the delicious laziness that was taking over.

"I'm getting hungry," muttered John. "Want to go out for a bite to eat?"

"Sure, we can do that," I replied, although hunger wasn't necessarily a sensation that was emphasized in me at the moment.

We got up then and started to change and get ready to go out. As I was combing my hair, I noticed that he had stopped for a second and was looking at my drawing on the bedside table. He didn't say anything, but smiled at the piece of paper and then, for a moment, turned his smile to me. And then he went back to his things once more. I held back a pang of disappointment, accepting his half-second smile as a form of congratulation. I was now more or less used to his near-null manifestations about my art.

When we were ready and about to leave the room, John hugged me tightly from behind, gently kissing the side of my neck. I smiled and enjoyed the shiver that his gesture gave me, already forgetting the micro frustration of moments ago. He had a way of making me feel so extraordinarily good that his faults left almost no void in me as if he could complete me even though he was so incomplete at times. Even after he released me, the sensations continued to throb in me, and as I descended the stairs and found myself once more in that wonderful house, I felt suddenly and could have sworn that I was the happiest person in the world at that instant.

"Are you going out, children?" We hadn't noticed his mother, who was reading a book sitting in an armchair in the living room.

"We're just going to get something to eat," replied John, "and I want to show Clara a little bit of the town."

"Enjoy! But don't eat too much, I want you both here for dinner."

"You got it." This time the answer came from me.

We said goodbye and went to the car. The day was still immensely beautiful, with a sun that shone in a different way than in New York City. It was probably because of the absence of the tall buildings and the thick layer of pollution that hung over the big city. I don't know. But the sky was bluer and the air was lighter. You could hear, even from inside the car, the sound of birds singing or the wind that moved the leaves on the trees. It was a melody that screamed in my ears and, at the same time, was so similar to the sounds of silence.

John started driving to places he wanted me to see. We stopped for a moment in a park overlooking a lake. The waters weren't very blue like the ones we have in Brazil, but the darkened tone seemed to blend in with the rest of the landscape in a perfect way. There were two or three boats in the distance, some children playing in the playground, a few people sitting on the benches with their iced coffees, and some walking or running around. A smaller, more open Central Park, I would say. With the difference that, in the case of the metropolis' park, as soon as one's feet reached the exit, one returned to the concrete city. Here, the park, the lake, they weren't an enclosure separated from the rest. The entirety of the small town was reflected there, and I found it such an incredible thing that I had to hold back some tears that wanted to express my affection for such a unique piece of beauty.

We ended up having lunch at a small Mexican restaurant near the park. From the window next to the table where we were sitting, I could see part of the lake. John told me he used to go there a lot when he lived in town and recommended chicken enchiladas, which I had with a traditional mojito. As usual, the huge portions of food from that country made me leave half of it on the plate, which I asked to pack for takeout. During our meal, as always, we didn't delve too deeply into conversations. He told me about his childhood and adolescence there, the familiar places, and everything that revolves around the subject.

After lunch, he drove around town with me some more. He showed me his old school, the square on the main street, the diner that, according to him, had the best pancakes ever... I was, as was often the case in this chapter of my existence, ecstatic with everything I saw. I thought of how vast this world is, and how little of it I knew and yet so much I had seen in my young life. I felt my heart warm if there is a way to express that feeling.

At the end of the day, we went back to his mother's house. There, dinner was waiting for us, so elaborate that I felt a little uncomfortable. We had drinks in the living room while we talked about things I had never experienced. Afterward, we went to the dining room to eat foods I had never had. It was comical to see myself there, in that huge house, eating duck and listening to them talk about problems with the jacuzzi, past trips to Europe, or how hard it was to find a good gardener. Surrealities that were almost part of my routine now. Or so I wished if I was being honest with myself. After dinner, we sat back in the living room, the TV playing a baseball game. They were both talking about sports, and I smiled every now and then as if I was paying full attention to what they were saying.

At night, we made love. Well, "love" is a strong word for the expression, actually. It was, as always, something between lovemaking and wild sex. Despite the now known movements, without much variety, almost like a script, sex was still an experience that bordered on the divine, connecting us in what seemed to be body, soul, and mind. Then came, invariably like everything else, the sleep of exhaustion.

The next day, we took advantage of the heat to spend most of the time in the pool. Beer and snacks were our food, and my outfits ranged from pajamas to bikini to pajamas. Nothing beats the doldrums of vacation idleness—feeling the heat of the sun on your face, the intoxication of alcohol at your core, and that generalized affection for life. With the conclusion that every day of that summer would be like this, I went to sleep happy that night. But the next dawn soon came, bringing with it clouds of rain that darkened the surroundings.

"Oh, that sucks," was the first thing John said when he woke up and saw me looking at the water crashing against the window.

"Yeah..." I replied only.

John got up, stretched, the usual. I continued watching the view. The rain was beautiful, despite its controversial nature. And I liked to look at beautiful things. I thought Dark Angel might also appreciate nature's simple enchantments. I definitely missed our conversations.

"Well," said John, snapping me out of my ramblings, "since it's raining, I thought maybe we could have lunch with my father. I want to introduce you two."

"Oh yes, great idea."

I had completely forgotten that his father also lived in town. I wondered if I would have gotten to know him if it hadn't been for the rain. Odd. Well, actually, nothing more common than the mother being the protagonist of her children's lives. In any case, whatever the reason was, I figured it was a good thing that I was getting to know a little bit more of John's life.

After an elaborate breakfast with his mother, he called his father, then arranged to meet him at a restaurant that, for the name, must be Italian. We spent the moments before the meeting talking trivially and strolling through the common areas of the house, not knowing what to do other than filling silences. After what seemed like an eternity, it was finally time to go.

The rain caught us a little on the way to the car and then from it to the entrance of the restaurant, but it didn't bother me. It was actually good to feel the icy drops touching me as if waking me up with their energy.

We sat at a table and waited. The place was very nice and cozy, almost like an Italian canteen. I ordered a soda, and John got a beer. We didn't talk much for a few good moments. I realized that I was more nervous than I thought, having no idea of what his father would be like. He hadn't told me much about him, and I hadn't stopped to wonder, which was a bit surprising since my mind always seemed to be fantasizing about everything. Anyway, before I could begin to conceive anything, John's father walked into the restaurant.

The moment I saw him, I knew it was him. His features were immensely similar to John's. Besides, there was something in the man's eyes that made his relationship to his son undeniable. As soon as he walked in, he spotted our table and walked over, a wide smile on his face. John stood up and they exchanged a loose but affectionate hug.

"Dad, this is Clara," he said, pointing at me. I got up and extended my hand to greet him. "Clara, this is my father, Robert."

"Nice to meet you," I said with an automatic smile.

"Likewise," he replied, also automatically, and sat down with us.

The first moments were awkward. The words of supposed interest escaped our lips, but the aura was one of discomfort. Between "What do you do?" and "Are you enjoying New York?" etc. etc., the silences were uncomfortable. The conversation, throughout the meal, did not go beyond the superficiality that was so much a part of everyday life. John ended up ordering another beer, and another, and another. His laughter became easier, and I started to worry a little. His father hadn't had anything but sparkling water. He pretended, as I did, that sobriety was not displeasing in the face of his son's increasingly evident drunkenness.

"John, don't you want to order some water?" he said at one point, as casually as he could, you could tell.

"Water?" Answered John, right after finishing the last drop of the beer in his glass. "No, I need one more." He then made a move to signal the waiter, but his arm stopped midway, blocked by his dad's hand.

"What is this?" John asked, his tone indignant and at a volume that caught the attention of a few people at nearby tables.

"You're driving, son," Robert replied softly as he released his arm.

"Yes, yes, yes, I know how responsible you are, right, pop?" John now wore, in keeping with his tone, an ironic smile. His eyes, however, held what appeared to be anguish—or pain, perhaps.

"John, let's not do this here, okay?" Robert looked from his son to me, apprehensive and clearly embarrassed.

"Why not? You don't want me to tell Clara that mom left you because of your drinking problem? Or maybe you don't want people around to know that you are an AA member?"

Robert closed his eyes for a moment, probably not knowing what to do with himself. He opened his mouth at one point, but it seemed like the words were stuck in his throat, and nothing was said in the end.

"John..." I started to say but I was interrupted by a laugh so sinister it was hard for me to believe it was coming from him.

"Oh, let's go, Clara. Waiter! Waiter! The check!"

The guy who served us quickly brought us our bill, certainly wanting to get rid of the problem we were becoming as quickly as possible. Robert tried to pay, but John aggressively refused. His father soon gave in, also notably wanting to end that encounter.

"I need to go to the bathroom," John said after the waiter had left to make the payment with his card. Then he staggered toward the restrooms, and I sat there with Robert in what felt like the most uncomfortable situation I'd ever been in.

"I'm sorry, Clara," he said after a few moments of awkward silence. "He doesn't usually drink that much. I want you to know that."

"I know. Don't worry."

"Do you guys need a ride? Or a taxi, perhaps?"

"No, I'll drive. Thanks."

Robert breathed a sigh of relief, the first positive emotion he'd manifested on that entire lunch. John didn't take long to return. He signed the receipt, left a tip, and took my arm gently to lead me out. Before we left, I reached out to his father.

"It was nice to meet you," I said, not knowing what other words could come out of my mouth that would make any sense.

"It was nice to meet you too." He replied, forcing a smile, which made him look sadder than before. And, turning to John, "Take care, son. We'll talk later."

John didn't respond. We got out of the restaurant, leaving his father behind—relief—and found it was raining even harder. When we got to the car, I took the keys from him, and he didn't protest. I hesitated. I hadn't driven in a while. The rain and the fact that I didn't know my way around the town hit me hard; my legs shook a little. I closed my fingers on the key tightly, ignored my body's signs of anxiety, and put it in the ignition. I put his mother's address into the GPS on my cell phone and drove us back, at last, on a journey of no more than twenty minutes—long stormy and chaotic minutes. But, in the end, we arrived at the house without major problems, except for the ones hiding inside me, protected by a facade of normality. Upon entering, we came across his mother, who was watching TV. She soon noticed her son's drunkenness, casting a scolding look in his direction.

"How was lunch?" she asked in a way that made her sound neutral.

John opened his mouth to start saying something, but I was quicker.

"It was good. But he ended up drinking a little too much." I chuckled casually as if telling an amusing anecdote. And, turning to John, "I think you'd better take a nap."

He didn't answer me but let himself be led to the room where we were staying. There, he threw himself on the bed and immediately fell asleep. I took off his shoes and turned him to his side so he would be more comfortable. Then I lay down next to him myself, finally managing to breathe. I thought about the events of lunch, even if I didn't want to. I relived the embarrassment, reflected on the new information I had about John's life. His father was an alcoholic then. I wasn't quite sure how to relate that fact to the rest of what I already knew about him. I didn't try too hard, though, turning more to my own issues. I remembered the fear of taking the steering wheel in my hands—control without control. My legs were still shaky. I wondered what I would do if I had to live in the American suburbs—no subways, no buses, no sidewalks in many cases. I mentally thanked the beloved and hated New York City for being my home.

My thoughts brought a few isolated tears to my eyes. I'm not sure why. I wasn't necessarily sad or distressed; it was just a lot. A lot to process all at once. Lots of accumulated things. I was emotionally tired. I closed my eyes for a moment, trying to fall asleep. Perhaps the relieved physical fatigue would give me some mental peace as well. But before I could rest, I felt my phone vibrate in my pants pocket. I thought about ignoring whatever the notification was, but my hand went to the device almost as if it had a life of its own. As soon as I unlocked the screen, my heart fluttered heavily. My friend Dark Angel had sent me a new email.

I sat up in the bed, now fully alert, opened the message quickly, already smiling even before I started reading. I don't think I'd ever been so happy to hear from him. The emotions of a few moments ago were now somewhere of shallow insignificance in the background of my mind. And, without dwelling on reasonings of ponderation or prudence, I began the avid reading of his email.

"Black Rose,

I'm sorry I haven't written you in a while. I've been working a lot—too much, in fact—and that has taken a toll on my health. I caught a really bad cold and, instead of taking care of myself, I continued to work, and it ended up becoming pneumonia. Anyway, I'm better now, but I had to put my phone and computer screens aside for a while; migraine was one of the symptoms of this illness and it is not fun at all.

Other than that, there's not much going on. More of the same, as always. Oh, except I bought a new painting. It's in my room, right above my bed's headboard. The style is similar to yours, although obviously nothing compares to your work. And don't worry: as soon as you decide to sell me one of your paintings, it will replace this one immediately.

How's it going over there? Enjoying the school break? Making the most of the summer? Hope everything is ok!

I miss your art. Any new ones? I hope you have time to produce something while you enjoy the time off.

Xoxo,
Dark Angel"

I read and reread his message—over and over and over. I'd been hungry. I intensely wanted someone who wished to know about my art, my life. No, not "someone"—him, my Dark Angel. An irresistible drug was the euphoria experienced whenever my "hunger" was sated. But sated wasn't the word, for I always wanted more. I was hopelessly addicted.

I got up from the bed and walked over to the little table that still held my last drawing. I took a picture of the paper with my cell phone to send it to my friend. But I didn't do it right away. Instead, I relished the fact that I was in control again. Now, he was the one waiting. And I wanted to feed that wait for his "hunger" to become as intense as my own. That sense of power was also addictive. Dark Angel supplied me with compulsive feelings and I let myself sink into all the little obsessions that came from him without any more fear of drowning in those dangerous waters.

I looked at John, so vulnerable in that particular moment. My excitement for our relationship had somewhat faded. I felt superior to him, in defiance of my judgment condemning the feeling. I felt that my dark angel was also superior, even though this comparison was acutely unfair. After all, Dark Angel had the advantage that his mundane aspects were, to me, a ghost. It was much easier to remain fascinated by a faceless specter.

I got a little tired of my own thoughts. So I decided to put aside the little games and answer my friend, after all. Suddenly, it didn't make much sense to keep him waiting, as that meant I would also suffer from the agony of waiting. After attaching the photo I had taken of my drawing to the email reply, I started typing.

"Dark Angel,

I was very happy to receive your message. I missed our conversations. I'm sorry you got sick. I know how complicated it is to remember to take care of yourself when so many other priorities (which shouldn't be) take over. But I'm glad you're better. Please take good care of your health.

I'm curious to see this painting you bought. You must have liked it a lot to have it decorating a place as intimate as your bedroom. And as for selling my art to you, even if I had reached the status of being able to market my paintings, I would never charge you.

Things are going fine here. I'm really enjoying my summer vacation. I was certainly missing the nice warmth I grew up with... even though it's sometimes difficult to live with the intense heat, I much prefer that than to deal with the cruel winter of this place.

As for producing, it's not much, but I made a drawing that I'm sending you. I'm trying not to put art aside, but at the same time, I want to enjoy my free time without too many obligations. Anyway, you never know when inspiration comes, right?

I hope you are enjoying the summer a little and that you manage not to let work be your center. Don't get sick again.

Xoxo,
Black Rose"

After sending the email, I thought about trying to sleep—naively, of course. Every atom in me felt the potency of my energetic existence. I didn't even want to lie down, actually. I went to the window to look at the rain for a moment, which continued to fall with the same intensity as before, oblivious to the particular storms that coexisted with it. Then I walked around the room not knowing what to do with myself, ruminating on the day's events and thinking about the near future. The next day would be our last there. I wondered if anything would change between me and John after what we'd shared on those summer days, after I entered his house, his childhood, even his family afflictions.

I also thought about the obscurity of not being with him all the time. Those few days had gotten me used to sleeping and waking up next to him, eating meals together, sharing every minute of the day with each other.

Suddenly, as my brain wandered through these corners of my mind, an inspired thought came to me. I went to the little table where the drawing I had just sent to my virtual friend was, detached a blank sheet of paper from the notebook I had used, and, with a black pen, started to draw. The shapes were flowing—natural, organic. And I saw the image when I finished the work: it was John lying in bed, eyes closed. Peaceful. Without knowing the knowledge that torments the human souls. For the first time, a drawing of mine portrayed a person who didn't live only in my imagination. I liked the illustration. There was passion there, which chose to blind itself. But I didn't want John to see it. For some mysterious reason. So I folded the sheet of paper and put it in my bag, which was hanging on a chair. Done. The End. In the nothingness of my bag...

After drawing or painting, the expected exhaustion always took over. It was as if my energy was suddenly channeled into that art, no longer in my body. And, of course, this time was no different. I went back to bed. I lay down next to John, hugged him from behind, closing my eyes, letting sleep slowly overtake me. Usually, the sleeping position was reversed, with him wrapping his arms around me. But I enjoyed being like that as if dominating the space that used to be his. And he, without choice, submitted. I'm not sure how much time passed, but before I knew it, I was already completely engulfed in a deep sleep. When I woke up, John was still wrapped in my arms, but I sensed he was awake. Realizing that I was moving slowly, he turned to me, now hugging me from the front, and kissed me gently on the forehead.

"Did you sleep well?" he whispered in a hoarse voice.

Not yet fully awake, eyes half-closed, I yawned before answering.

"Yes, and you?"

"Yes, I completely blacked out."

We lay there for a while not saying anything, just looking at each other. And the look in his eyes, I realized, was one of shame—I don't know whether from the drunkenness itself, or from his father, or both. I ran my fingers over his face sweetly, smiled. I wanted to assure him that everything was fine.

"Any trace of a hangover?" I asked, trying to bring some lightness to the moment.

"Oh, I'm just very thirsty. And I still feel like I'm a little dizzy, but at least I don't have a headache or anything."

"That's good. Let's go downstairs, then, get some water, and spend the rest of the day with your mother."

John smiled gratefully. Perhaps he was expecting to find an angry or disappointed Clara upon waking. But, oddly enough, I was actually almost happy. The fact that I saw him so vulnerable, in a moment of lack of control and in the middle of a family drama, made me feel closer to him.

"I'm sorry about what happened," he said, his smile fading and his expression turning to regret.

"I understand. These things happen."

"I want you to know that I don't drink like that all the time. Even though my dad... I don't have a drinking problem."

"I know that."

He kissed my lips softly, and the matter was closed. The rain had almost completely stopped, although some stubborn drops still insisted on falling. We got out of bed and went about the day. When we got downstairs, we found a smiling Dorothy.

"Hi, children! Did you sleep well?"

"Like babies," I replied.

"If one of the babies was drunk," John added with a chuckle, which soon spread to us.

"Well, you're on vacation. It happens," his mother said. And a little more serious now, "But let's try to control ourselves, shall we?"

"Right," replied her son, eyes downcast.

No surprise that any trace of what could turn out to be alcoholism in her own child would terrify this woman, who had undoubtedly had her share of martyrdom in dealing with her ex-husband. Nothing more was said about the incident, however. We spent the rest of the day talking about trivialities and how sad she was that we were leaving so soon. We ordered Japanese food for dinner and then sat in the living room sipping wine while the TV entertained us with a reality show about a chef competition. Actually, John preferred to only drink water, but I enjoyed the slight intoxication and the sweet taste of my drink, giving in to the state of relaxation provided by the nectar of Dionysus.

At one point, we decided to call it a night. Dorothy was clearly sleepy, occasionally closing her eyes right there on the couch. John and I, on the other hand, were still wide awake, probably from our long nap not long ago. In any case, we went to the bedroom. Once there, I started to open the small suitcase I had brought with the intention to begin packing for the next day, as we were planning to leave right after breakfast. However, I was interrupted by John, who grabbed me by the waist, lifting my feet off the ground, making me laugh with pleasure. He carried me to the bed and showered my face with smacking kisses. We were both laughing with tickles and also, of course, for the joy of that moment.

The kisses soon became more intense and the laughter turned to hoarse moans, and our bodies, once again, joined in a choreographic dance of purity and pleasure. The pleasant slowness followed the easy satisfaction, and we stayed there enjoying the sensations of the delicious softness, hugging in a perfect fit. I wouldn't have chosen, at that moment, to be anywhere else in the world.

"How are you feeling?" asked John suddenly, which surprised me greatly. It was the first time he had ever asked me that.

"I am great. And you?"

"Me too."

I kept waiting for him to add something to that unusual dialogue, but what followed was the silence of before. I, for my part, had nothing to say either. But I thought for a long time about the reason for such a question. I don't know if he was referring to the physical aspect of what we had just experienced or if he wanted to know about my emotions and feelings. But my answer covered both meanings. My body and my mind and my soul were perfectly harmonized in an atmosphere of satisfaction.

The reflecting time passed quickly and I realized that John had fallen asleep again. I looked at the time on my phone—half-past twelve. I checked my email, but there was still no response from my virtual friend. I checked social media too but saw nothing but more of the same. It was funny how the sameness managed to entertain me, though. Especially the things that made me laugh. My eyes, glued to the screen, didn't close until nearly two in the morning. And even after that, my sleep was interrupted several times. More tossing and turning in bed than actual sleep that night. When I realized the sun was rising once more.

Deciding not to try in vain to fall asleep again, I let myself wake up for good. With an automatic movement, I picked up my phone once more, intending to go back to memes and photos and thoughts of my friends, but I was surprised by an email from Dark Angel. He had just written and, as usual, my heart stopped for a second, then returned to throbbing with the familiar passionate intensity. I opened his message without hesitation.

"Black Rose,

I missed our conversations too. Immensely. It would have been so much easier to get through this irritating illness if I'd had the solace of your virtual company. But the important thing is that we are now back to normal. It's funny how I can barely remember a time before our friendship. I feel like you've been around my whole life.

Don't worry, I've learned my lesson. I will no longer let anything come before my health. Much less work. How easy it is, however, to prioritize our livelihood...

I took a picture of the painting and am sending it to you. As I said, it's not a Black Rose original, but I really liked it. It's been good for me to have this piece of art so close, to be able to appreciate its beauty before I go to sleep and when I wake up. And once you sell me your painting (I would never not pay for such incredible work), as I said too, it will be my daily admiration.

I'm glad you're enjoying the warm weather. From the looks of it, you're from a warmer place. I must confess that I prefer the cold. Go figure, right?

As always, your art brought me immense content-ment. It's unbelievable what you can do with so few supplies. A piece of paper, a pen, and that's it—a masterpiece. The complexity of art created in the

purest simplicity. How I wish I had a gift as unbe-
lievably fantastic as yours. Be proud of yourself!

My summer is certainly not being as well spent
as yours, but I'm definitely letting work be what it
is—work. That's something. And as for not getting
sick, I promise to try my best.

Xoxo,
Dark Angel"

Ah, how those words nourished my being! A few scribbles on a piece of paper became a masterpiece in his eyes. Where else would I have this? Certainly not from John. Not with such enthusiasm from my friends. My dark angel was the only one capable of providing me with such affection of my own ego. I basked in the sensation for a good few minutes. Then, I remembered to open the attached photo of the painting that adorned his room. The picture framed the painting, but I could see part of the wall as well. It was one of those textured ones, and it had a dark color—brown or black, I couldn't see it well in the photo—and it contrasted greatly with the painting itself, which contained lighter shades. I had a slightly strange feeling discovering this tiny fraction of the surroundings of my friend's life. I had entered his room, where he slept, where he made love and contemplated beauties and dreamed.

As for the art itself, it depicted a piece of nature in the winter. Trees with their dry branches, some snow here and there. The painting was very beautiful. It reminded me a little of that first drawing that I had posted on the blog that was now completely abandoned. I wondered if he had unconsciously chosen that painting because of that. Or, who knows, maybe he did it consciously. In any case, it made me happy to imagine his motives.

Before I could even attempt to respond to his email, John suddenly woke up, turning to my side and stretching for a long time. I set my phone aside on the nightstand and smiled at him.

"Good morning," I said enthusiastically.

"Good morning," he replied, between a yawn and another. "Someone woke up in a good mood."

My euphoric delight was then quite evident. I tried to contain it a little—the why shrouded in mystery—although without much success.

"Yeah, I had a good night's sleep," I lied.

"I slept very well too," he replied, closing his eyes and yawning once more.

I observed his face, still puffy from sleep, and how his muscles contracted as he opened up his arms and stretched with pleasure. Even after all that time together, I still hadn't gotten used to his handsomeness so wrapped in harmony and grandeur.

"What?" asked John when he saw my eyes on him.

"Oh, nothing..." I replied casually. And, changing the subject, "We better start getting ready to go, huh?"

Still without much energy, he got up and went to the bathroom while I started to pack our things. A kind of animosity began to creep over me at the prospect of the near future, when I would be in my apartment with Kat and see John only on weekends and, when classes resumed, for a few mornings a week. I tried to push the thought away, but the feeling continued to surround me. Even when I smiled gratefully at his mother for her hospitality as we said our goodbyes or when I enjoyed the sights on the way back or when I laughed at some joke John told in the car, the feeling of strangeness, even anguish, remained.

It didn't take long for the tall, gray buildings to appear through the window again. Now the honking, the police sirens, the people talking loudly hurt my ears almost deafeningly. The traffic lights, the car lights, the streetlamps and buildings, and the pollution were all too obvious, and I wondered if it was even possible that this was the place I called home.

Before returning the rental car, John dropped me off at home. He parked in front of the building and kissed me tenderly on the lips. A light, affectionate touch.

"Thanks for coming with me. I had a great time," he said, flashing a smile that harmonized with the serene kiss of a moment ago.

"No, thank you," I replied, trying to find that aura of tranquility that emanated from him—without success. The anguish of coming back to reality was still very much alive in me.

"I'm sorry again for...you know." His voice was still soft, but his face twitched a few inches, still very likely carrying the shame of the fateful episode with his father.

"No, no more apologies, please," I replied while caressing his face. "I had a great time and I loved visiting your hometown."

His smile returned to its usual lull, and, without a word, we got out of the car to get my things from the trunk. We said goodbye once more and I went on my way to real life. Still in the elevator, I already began to feel the agony of loneliness intensifying. I didn't want to leave him. I wanted to call him and propose that we'd go to dinner that same day and that he'd sleep next to me again, even if in my tiny bed. And that we'd spend the next day together as well. And...

The elevator door opened and I dragged myself to my apartment. Kat greeted me with a friendly smile, to which I responded with a smile also as if there wasn't a longing taking over my soul.

"You're back!" she said enthusiastically. "How was the trip?"

"Oh, it was amazing!" I replied, dropping my stuff somewhere and sitting next to her on the couch. I spent a good half hour there recounting details of the experience, omitting, of course, the incident with John's father.

"And how have your days been?" I asked after finishing my narrative.

"Oh, the usual," she replied with a bored expression. "Work, bars, guys..."

After we exchanged news, the conversation soon died down. It was then replaced by television entertainment, which we enjoyed for hours on end. When it was almost nighttime, I had something to eat and then went to the solitude of my room—which I tried so hard to put off, but eventually, eventually, there is no way out. John hadn't sent me anything—and, naively, I'd expected some...something—and loneliness felt like a weight on my shoulders again. And in order to heal myself a bit, I decided to respond to Dark Angel's latest email. I opened the inbox on my phone, but for a second I couldn't find his message. I don't know if my eyes were playing tricks on me or if the app was having a problem. My breath stopped for a moment and I felt, there, how great was the fear of losing him.

I closed the app and opened it again. The relief of discovering that his email was still there was so powerful that I almost laughed. And almost cried. Everything at the same time. I noticed that the fingers I used to open the message were sweating. I pulled myself together as best I could, all too aware of how ridiculous my reaction was. I suddenly found myself watching the person I had been these past few days—or was it months? My own company didn't seem to be enough anymore and I yearned for...something. My attention went from John to Dark Angel to John again to Dark Angel again. This neutral being who looked at me from within concluded that this dynamic could not be healthy. But I let it be just a voice in the back of my thoughts. Almost inaudible, I decided. I then turned once more to the task of answering my friend. Shutting myself up.

"Dark Angel,

I have the same feeling that there is no pre-you time. And I keep imagining that there isn't a future after you either. Too deep? Sorry, I'm a little contemplative. Anyway, I'm glad we have the present time, which is enough for me. And obviously, I'm glad you're willing to take better care of yourself. It's really easy to prioritize work when it should only be a small (and irritating, I would say) part of our existence.

I really like the painting you bought. Your eye for art is amazing. Selfishly, this fact makes me very pleased that you appreciate my work. Who knows, maybe one day there might be a painting of mine in your room?

Yes, I'm from a very hot place. I can't get used to the cold in this country. But I suppose it has its good side. At least we can count on heaters in these modern times (I wonder what it was like before such technology and if I would survive on fireplaces alone).

You don't know how glad I am that you appreciate my art, even if it's just a scribbled piece of paper. As I've told you a few times, this appreciation motivates me to keep creating.

Well, I hope the rest of your summer is peaceful and that you can, in fact, put work aside a little.

Xoxo,
Black Rose"

I was a bit tired, not sure whether physically or emotionally. My mind hovered between opposing ideas and contradictory perceptions, but I desperately tried to silence it, which I actually was able to do with some success. However, there was still something draining my strength. I lay on my bed, putting the phone away. I thought about getting up and drawing or painting, but the truth is that I just wanted not to be at that moment.

I closed my eyes, and when I opened them again, I wasn't sure whether or not I had fallen asleep. But it was daytime. And it was Monday. Classes hadn't started yet, but I needed to get back to work. I missed my baby. It was surreal to be the person who followed her growth so closely. Her babbling words grew in meaning and her hesitant little steps soon turned into running and dancing and jumping. The work was not easy, but it was certainly worth it.

I didn't want to get up right away. I enjoyed the laziness, idleness that renewed my energy, so dense the night before. I picked up my cell phone while still lying down. For the first time in a while, I didn't go straight to my email or text messages, expecting news from John or Dark Angel. I logged into my section of the university's website to see my grades for that semester—all as expected. The contentment with my performance flattered me. Suddenly, a new text notification. It was John. I openly smiled, taken by pleasure, and went to see what he was saying.

"Hey, Clara! Thanks again for the trip. How are you doing?"

How good the false sensation of a rosy universe was; even if only for a few seconds. It was as if there were no more problems—mine, or the world's. I responded immediately.

"Hi, John! No, thank you! I'm fine, and you?"

Funny how easily the focus inside my head shifted, and how much the thoughts reflected on the rest of me—on my senses and physical sensations even. Sometimes I was disgusted by the ills of society, and sometimes—now—I had an infinite affection for humanity. It seemed to me, suddenly, that nothing but love emanated from the Earth.

245

The reflections were once again interrupted by John.

"I'm fine, too. A drag going back to work, tho. Want to do something this weekend?"

Ah, the weight of the wounds leaving me! The colors of delight taking over! How easy it was to live in that instant!

"Yeah, I'll be back to work later today too. I do, see you this weekend."

His response, almost instantaneous, consisted of a smiley face. Even his lack of words was dear to me now. And with this cloud of tenderness surrounding my aura, I got up to start my day. From everyday actions, like brushing my teeth, drinking coffee, to the most tender events, like seeing my baby, who welcomed me back with a loving smile at work, the day went on smoothly.

At night when I got home, I was tired but happy. Kat was in her room and, from the suspicious noises coming from there, it seemed she was not alone. I went to the kitchen to get something to eat. Lately, my diet consisted of frozen foods, widely available throughout that country—the harmful but resigned convenience. After my microwave meal, I went to my room. It was close to Kat's, which meant the sounds coming from there would be clearer, but, I reasoned, better than taking the risk of being in the living room and running into a random guy and having to talk about the weather with someone in his underwear. In any case, when I got to my bedroom, I put on my headphones and listened to music while wasting time looking at social media and internet banalities.

I quickly checked my email, but there was still no response from Dark Angel to my last message. I thought a lot about my friend and then about John. There weren't many other people lately. My closest and oldest friends were in Brazil. I had my baby, of course, but at the end of the day, I would give her back to her mother and finish my workday. Loneliness was difficult, and because of that, I was grateful for any affection that came my way. I took the headphones off, and there were no more sounds coming from the next room. I sighed in relief, as dormancy already started gracing me with its presence. It didn't take me long to fall asleep.

The days that week weren't much different from my Monday—lazy mornings, working afternoons, and nights spent coexisting with Kat's pleasures, who, apparently, was free from the social chains she used to let herself into. I don't know if she was seeing someone specific or different people, but either way, she seemed content. And I was prudently happy for her; it is difficult to differentiate whether some behaviors have to do with release or restlessness. Other than that, everything was more or less normal. On Friday, I finally got a reply from Dark Angel. I was on my way back from work when I saw the notification. I opened the email on the subway, my heart fluttering slightly.

"Black Rose,
Never apologize for such spontaneous reflections. I also can't imagine a future without you existing in it. It's a little frightening, but for now, I try not to think about it too much (as you said, the present is already a delight).

I'm definitely taking more care of myself, yes. I can no longer prioritize the banalest parts of existence so much, in fact. I hope you are doing the same.

I'm glad you liked the painting I got. If you appreciate my opinion on the matter, the opposite is even more true. After all, your view comes from the other side of the thing. I just observe; you create. And believe me, at the first opportunity, I want to have one of your originals in my house, without a doubt.

Are you from another country? Wow, I would have never guessed. Your English is excellent (I assume it's your second language?). Anyway, I hope you adapt to the sometimes harsh winter here. Before heaters, I don't even know if I myself would have survived it.

A scribbled paper is definitely not how I would describe anything I've ever seen you produce. I am extremely happy that you are motivated to continue creating your art and if it's up to me you will always have someone who appreciates it.

I hope things are going well with you. I want you to know that even though our contact is (questionably) superficial, I do care about you.

Xoxo,
Dark Angel"

It felt good to get nourished by his words. Although it was now part of my routine to have my ego graced by his messages, every time I got a new email, it still felt almost the same—sheer ecstasy. I decided to answer him right away, however, I was interrupted by a text from John.

"My day was chaotic. Can I stop by your place? I have wine."

How fortunate I was, and I knew it. I couldn't help but smile. More. I was already looking forward to the weekend to see him, and now I would have him even earlier than expected—how magical that connection! I closed my email inbox and then responded to him.

"Of course, I would love to see you. I'll be home in ten minutes."

He replied with an "ok"—brief, full, whole—and I already started the plans for the night while harboring all kinds of thoughts. Getting home, taking a quick shower, ordering something to eat, having dinner, watching a movie, drinking wine and chatting through the night, making love. And I, who was still feeling the deprivation of sleeping and waking up next to John, I longed for the moment that was approaching like a tired body waiting for the comfort of a warm bed.

It didn't take me long to get home. Kat wasn't there, and since it was Friday, I figured she'd be gone for a while. The shower and the getting ready and the tidying up of the apartment, especially messy that day, was quick, half frantic, avid. And soon I didn't have time to think about the rest, because John was now at my door.

We hugged for a long time as soon as we saw each other. He held me tightly in his arms, kissed my forehead several times. Not that he wasn't an affectionate person, but I found such eagerness in his gestures a little strange.

"Is everything all right?" I asked when we parted.

"Yes, just work problems," he replied evasively. "I'm happy to see you."

I smiled in contentment. He was happy to see me, happy as I was—and we sat down on the couch. I opened the bottle of wine he had brought and we chatted while sipping on it. We talked a little about work and the prospects of going back to school soon and other trifles. As the wine was savored, the words became looser and the volume of the conversation and the easy laughter that came from it grew louder. We even forgot that we were supposed to have dinner.

After a while, the talking died away, although the laughter was still present. Without much thought, in a silent mutual agreement, the conversation ceased, and came the kisses and caresses that, with every second, it seemed, became more intense. My being, which was only sensations at that moment, let me be carried away by his touch, his smell, his taste—and they left me almost in a state of fever, of hunger. His urgent hands roamed my body now, trying to free me of my clothes. When I was almost naked, the desire consuming me entirely, we were suddenly interrupted by the sound of the door opening.

Kat was visibly drunk. She staggered for a few seconds before even noticing our presence. When her eyes found us, she was speechless for a moment, then burst out laughing.

"Oops, sorry, guys, I didn't know you'd be here," she said, still chuckling, her voice wavering.

I tried to cover myself as much as I could and John jumped up on the couch, freeing me from his arms.

"No, we are sorry," I replied while still struggling to hide my nudity. "We should have gone to the bedroom."

Kat didn't respond, but continued her laughter and, to my surprise, walked over to where we were, sitting between me and John on the couch.

"Oh, there's no problem..." she said "you are both beautiful, you can do whatever you want. You can even include me if you want."

And she burst into laughter once more, gesturing as if to hug John; but I restrained her gently and got her to get up, leading her to her bedroom. I had given up on my clothes at that point and guided her to bed with difficulty, as I wasn't one hundred percent sober myself. As soon as she lay down, she immediately fell asleep. I then returned to the living room.

"Sorry, I didn't think she'd act like that," I said as I grabbed my clothes and walked to my room, followed by him.

"No need to apologize," he replied. His tone, I couldn't quite identify it.

When I closed the bedroom door, John took me in his arms eagerly, leading us to the bed soon after. He seemed even hungrier, kissing and squeezing me anxiously. It didn't take too long. It was an avid, savage sex. When we came, I was exhausted and we fell into a deep sleep in each other's arms.

The next day came softly, gently waking me up. I opened my eyes slowly and smiled to find

John still sleeping. I got up carefully so as not to wake him and went to make some coffee. I found Kat in the kitchen, slurping a glass of water. Seeing me, she put it aside and, with downcast eyes, said, "Clara, I'm so very sorry for yesterday! I'm so ashamed of my behavior."

I smiled at her and promptly replied, "You don't need to apologize. You were drunk; it's okay. We are the ones who shouldn't have been in a common area of the house."

"I hope you guys are not mad at me. I don't ever want to make you feel uncomfortable or disrespected."

"Kat, seriously, it's okay."

"You're the best!"

She hugged me for a moment and then went back to her water. I started making the coffee, and as I waited for the coffee maker to do its work, I heard footsteps coming from my room. It was John, of course, who soon joined us, greeting us with a general good morning, still sleepy. Kat also apologized to him, who assured her that everything was fine. Still, with the matter settled, you could feel a strangeness in the air, a hint of discomfort. But there was nothing we could do about it, and hopelessly, we just got on with our day. John ended up spending the entire weekend with me. And Kat was hardly home these days. She always had parties to go to or friends to meet, and her absence helped a little, at last, to assuage the aura that the Friday night situation had left.

In any case, from that day on, even if unconsciously, I avoided taking him home; instead, I'd rather we stayed at his apartment. And we did—every weekend for the rest of that summer. And on weekdays, I continued to exchange emails with Dark Angel. And things followed more or less this same routine of happiness (clean, genuine) for a while—a time when I lived the joy of good fortune, without thinking much about the after. However, when the leaves began to dry and the weather began to change, taking away the heat and bringing a little cold air to the surroundings, things also ended up transmuting in a way that that world, once stable, now changed in an invariable manner, just as the leaf that falls to the ground no longer shows its colors at the top of the tree.

Fall

The season's change barely arrived, and I already knew that fall would be my favorite one. Walking through Central Park those days was like walking through a literal daydream of perfection. The dry leaves formed a yellowish-red carpet that covered the entire floor as far as the eye could see. The intense heat was gone, but the sun still reigned most of the time, sharing the space with the occasional icy blast that the wind brought. Things changed in flavors. It was apples and pumpkins season, and the coffees, pies, bread, and everything else had a very distinctive taste. People were preparing for Halloween and, soon after, for Thanksgiving in November, a celebration so big in the country that it even competed with Christmas. We could already see many decorated pumpkins adorning houses and shops. And one of the best feelings in the world was breathing in the autumn air in the early hours of the morning when I left for college.

It was a little difficult to get back to the routine of class and work at first, but soon, as we are taught, I had adapted to the new-old reality. In any case, the good side of seeing John during the week made up for the tribulations of daily life. And we were getting closer and closer. Although we had never talked about it concretely, I now considered that we were in an official relationship. When I spoke of him in conversation with someone, I always referred to John as my boyfriend, for example. More than the silences that surrounded us, the gestures and habits, and affections of our relationship were enough for me.

Speaking of John, the first few weeks of school were difficult for him. He was showing up late almost every day. Apparently his job was demanding more and more of him, as work often does. So, therefore, our interaction in the time we shared in college was far less than I would have liked. However, as if to make up for some voids, another person was more present in my life in that environment: Alex. When we returned from summer vacation, as we both always arrived early at the university, we ended up spending time chatting, and, little by little, our bond increased.

There was also work. Although tiring, it was going well. The baby grew as fast as the seasons changed, and I had to adapt to her daily changes—which gave her more and more energy and made me more and more tired at the end of the day. But it was, even so, greatly rewarding to follow that growth—even with exhaustion taking over me because of the busy days, the games, the constant inventing of new activities to entertain her, the concern for her development—as strong as the love carried in my life, even though our ties were, technically, strictly professional.

And, of course, I continued to exchange emails with Dark Angel. Our relationship was also moving faster than I'd anticipated—if it had even crossed my mind that it was going anywhere at all. He already knew, by now, of my very Brazilian origins, which led to cultural questions and comparisons, and intimacies of my past, my tastes, my family... and the parallels and correlations of these aspects of myself with his own life and culture made so that he would also open up more. One day, almost as a joke, he asked my name. I changed the subject and he silenced his curiosity, but I had to reflect on how much I was willing to let him into my real life. And the truth is, I didn't have a definitive answer to that question—and I didn't necessarily want to.

So went my days. If I was not at school, I was at work, and, when home, busying myself with classwork or household chores. What little free time I had, I spent either texting John, or emailing Dark Angel. When there were no new messages, I entertained myself by reading old ones. It had been a while since I read a book or worked on any new art, although my dark angel always insisted that I'd get back into creating. I would tell him I didn't have time, which was partially true, but, in the most absorbed reality, the one that I didn't admit to myself, I was unwilling to do anything that minimally felt like working even more. Kat continued her routine of alternating work with partying, and otherwise, the world kept spinning, as usual.

On one of those ordinary days, I was sitting in the classroom waiting for the teacher to arrive while scribbling on my notebook. Suddenly, I was jolted out of my boring daze by a touch on the arm. It was John, who, for the first time in a long time, was on time for class.

"Hey, you're not late today!" I said smiling as he sat in the chair right next to mine.

"Yeah, I can't believe I woke up early," he replied, then kissed me on the cheek in greeting.

Before we could say anything else, the teacher arrived, and, barely putting his things on the table, he began the class—and announced, at one point, a project that would be worth nearly half of the term's grade. The work consisted of choosing a Human Resources theory and what it would be like to put it into practice in a fictitious company that we would create. The conclusions and thoughts formally written in the academic's norms, of course—the task would be done in pairs.

At the end of class, John, as he had been doing in recent days, said he needed to run, not without first proposing that we did the project together, and I, who hadn't even considered working on it with anyone else actually, obviously agreed. Which was almost funny. John was smart, sure, but negligent about college stuff. I wasn't even sure he'd pass all the classes. But obviously, the prospect of spending even more time with him was overpowering—by far. In the narrow seconds before his departure, then, we decided to start work as early as the following weekend. Or rather, I decided. And it was still Monday, and the promise of us getting together was already pulsing with anxiety in me, as usual. For now, though, texting was enough—fragments of his company, feeding me the crumbs that pleased and sickened me.

That week dragged on. That happened every time I had the prospect of seeing John. Now, even more. Lately, since we'd come back to school, we haven't seen each other every single weekend. He was busy—too much work. But it made me proud that he was so dedicated to his professional life. Every little thing he did caused me to admire him more and more. I wasn't used to reverencing a guy I was dating. It was refreshing to be with someone who had passions and commitments and ambitions—even if I was consequently not a priority for his intentions.

In any case, though painfully slow, the week came to its inevitable end. Saturday arrived, the day we planned to meet up at my place. Kat was out of town, completing the perfect backdrop for our intellectual seclusion. Although we didn't agree on a time, I assumed he would be early. I didn't consider his familiar frivolity with school. The hours passed, and he still wasn't there with me. I didn't want to bother him with text messages. We didn't even agree on an exact time; it was silly to yearn for what were just my expectations. I waited. I got the computer ready, jotted down some ideas. I stopped to eat. I turned on the TV. Turned off the TV. I fiddled with my cell phone. I went back to jotting down ideas. Finally, when it was almost eight o'clock, I decided to question him.

"Hey, are you still coming?"

The message seemed casual, I thought. You couldn't even tell that I had spent all the hours of that day waiting, waiting... I stared at my cell phone screen for a good five minutes. Then I put it aside and turned on the television once more. The news was on. I switched channels until I found a popular sitcom from the nineties that always distracted me. After about ten minutes, the notification came, making my heart race.

"Sorry, Clara, I was really busy today. May I go now?"

Oh, the calmness! So sweet, so easy.

"Sure, no problem."

I continued watching TV, now a delicious lightness, as if I was melting. John didn't take long to arrive. I received him with an eager grip, allowing myself to dissolve in his arms, which enveloped me with affection. We didn't start the project; I didn't care. We didn't talk much. I didn't ask about his day, nor he about mine. The hugs and squeezes and kisses led us to my bed. That night, I didn't come, but it did not matter. The experience of sex with John was different now. More... spiritual. The sexual desire was in the background. We soon fell asleep.

I woke up the next day; he was not by my side. I heard the noise of the television in the living room, and concluded that he had woken up early and didn't want to disturb me. I was touched by his care. I smiled to myself, enjoying the sensation, making a conscious effort not to laugh with pleasure. I didn't want him to hear it, to know it. Finally, I got up, put on something comfortable to cover my nakedness, grabbed my computer, and also a notebook, and headed to the living room. Upon seeing me, John turned off the TV.

"I thought we'd get to work," I said, sitting down next to him and turning on the laptop.

"Yes, that's a good idea." he replied. "It's great that you're responsible like that, because, if it was up to me, we would never start."

"I'm a little lazy too." I wanted to be sympathetic.

"Don't you want coffee first?"

I nodded, and he headed for the kitchen. Although the coffee maker did the work itself, he lingered there until the coffee powder morphed, exhaling its morning scent throughout the apartment. As slowly as possible, it seemed to me, he poured the drink into the cup, sweetened it, stirred it with the spoon, stirred... when there was nothing more to do, he returned to the living room, at last.

I grabbed my coffee, opened the laptop as fast as he was slow. I accessed some files on the computer with articles on subjects that I found interesting, then took the notebook and a pen.

"I thought we could write down ideas and then organize what we want to do; we should plan a schedule so as not to miss the deadline and designate what each one is responsible for doing."

He nodded. I showed him the articles and subjects that I liked and quickly started talking about the ideas I already had.

"Basically, I think we should talk about diversity in the workplace. I thought of simulating how a company that had an inclusion policy in hiring employees would work."

Was there a certain passion in my speech? Yes, I noticed the flame, even though it was still weak, that was kindled somewhere in me. And the contentment that came with the discovery, because I invariably found myself thinking about how I didn't necessarily love that field. But who would have thought that there could be an opportunity there to build a better world? My work could, after all, be relevant to society.

"Yes, that's a good idea," John replied. I came out of my epiphanic ecstasy to meet what appeared to be a bored man and also one that was glad I was taking the reins of the project.

I continued, "I thought at first that we could talk about the thing in general, but I think that if we get more specific, we can really focus on the problems faced by a particular group, as each minority has its particularities when it comes to getting a job."

John nodded and waited for me to continue. He took a sip of my coffee—for some reason, he hadn't brought his own cup—and yawned.

"Well, my first thought was for women, obviously. You know, not being hired because of the possibility of getting pregnant or the issue of having children or not, the lower salary... but despite it still being very bad, there are people talking about it and a discussion is definitely going on."

"Wow, you really thought about it, didn't you?" John interrupted me.

"Well, I... live it."

He was silent, keeping to himself what he thought or felt. And I couldn't read his depths in the neutral expression of his face. I then continued.

"Anyway, I thought we could talk about something relevant that wasn't being discussed so widely yet. How do you feel about working on implementing policies for transgender people in our fictional company?"

John was silent for a few moments. He had been perfecting the art of reticence, wary in his stillness. But this time, clear as water untouched by man, his face was one of doubt.

"Oh, well, I... I don't know. I can't even imagine where we would start."

"Yeah, I know. And that is precisely part of the problem. I don't think anyone thinks about this, least of all employers."

He still hesitated, one could tell. I didn't understand why it was such a difficult thing to accept. In my mind, it sounded like a great idea, and I even thought about talking to Alex to get a clearer sense of what were the biggest problems this population faced in the job market. I waited for his resolution for a few moments but got nothing.

"John? What do you think?"

After a few more moments of uncertainty, he finally replied, "If you think we can do it, I'm in. We can talk about it, yes."

So I started making notes with topics that I thought were relevant for us to cover, as well as research methods and a draft of our schedule. I scribbled nonstop, an enthusiasm long lost to the erratic notions of the academic world, and its afterward. John just accepted everything I suggested, without giving an opinion or proposing anything new. Nor did he offer himself for the practical part of the thing, writing or typing or...

Once we were done, it was lunchtime, and he suggested we'd go out to eat. I went to change my clothes, and as I was getting ready, a singular, strange feeling came over me. 'He doesn't care about the project,' was the thought that ran through my head, unmistakable. But more importantly, 'He doesn't care about what I said regarding inclusion and minorities.' No, no, he has to care. He just never stopped to think about it. Of course. But I will have to be responsible for the execution of the work as much as I was for its idealization. Ah, thoughts that I didn't invite didn't stop floating before my naivety. He would help me, yes. With the project. With everything. Not with the details, no, but it didn't matter. I wanted to chase my thoughts away, but there was a price to pay for delving into someone.

At lunch at a nearby diner, as we ate, he told me about how busy and stressful his Saturday had been. And how happy he was to be with me today. Done. All the strangeness from before, the doubts and anxieties evaporated. All was right, after all. He wasn't very socially sensitive, not a big deal. I knew he was invariably a good person. And after working so hard, especially on a Saturday, I was flattered to be the one who made his day brighter.

We finished our meal, paid the bill. I was going to ask him if he wanted to see a movie or have ice cream, but before I could, he pulled his cell phone out of his pocket while saying, "Wow, there are almost no cars available on the app today."

I was silent for a few moments, not understanding well. Would he leave already? It was just after two in the afternoon. I wanted to question his whys, but instead, I smiled awkwardly and, as naturally as possible, replied, "Wow, how strange."

He didn't answer me, still with his eyes glued to the screen of his device. A glimmer of a smile took over his face for a second.

"Oh, I got one! It arrives in five minutes."

My expression was one of informality. Natural, laid-back. I commented again about how unusual it was for there not to be that many drivers at that time of day. Perhaps there was some event nearby that we were not aware of. And the weather was good, it wasn't raining or anything. Good thing he'd found one, anyway. But whatever, we would order a taxi if anything.

The five minutes passed with unusual haste. His driver was waiting for him outside. I left the diner walking beside him, arms touching. I longed to hold his hand on the short walk to the car, but I didn't. He kissed me on the cheek. I smiled. He got in. Left me.

I walked back to the apartment, a little dazed, a little aimlessly. I mean, I knew where my feet took me, of course. But that was it. I looked at my cell phone, foolishly hoping he'd texted me explaining himself. Saying he had to leave early because of work. 'But screw work, I'm coming back to you, Clara. The car is turning around, wait for me in front of your building. Let's have ice cream, the pistachio one, your favorite, and then watch a horror movie.' But the black screen of the device gave me nothing.

In the elevator of the building, I couldn't contain a few lonely tears. Well, what nonsense! He didn't need to spend every second with me. In fact, I didn't even want a kind of relationship with such codependency. I was an independent woman, and he was also a free man. Two complete individuals. Except for the fact that I didn't feel complete in that lonely elevator. I looked at myself in the mirror, which reflected a somewhat different Clara from the one who had started that journey in the United States. I still had dreams. But they had now changed without my realizing it. My dreams met them. Him. If there were unseen forces somewhere, I would ask them, more than anything, for John to be there. I would beg them for him to be there.

I arrived at the empty apartment, and suddenly felt uninhabited. Alone. I thought about starting my part of the project but couldn't concentrate right now. I turned on the television, but the images and sounds coming from the screen made no sense. My eyes went to my cell phone all the time, waiting... I opened the chat with John, thought about sending something. But what? I closed the messaging app at last, as I didn't know what to say to him. I went to my email then. And without much thought, I started writing.

"Dark Angel,

How have you been? My weekend has been a little... sad. To tell you the truth, I'm feeling a bit lonely and I didn't know who to talk to. I hope you don't mind reading my rant.

I have a thousand things to do from college but can't focus on what's important right now. Ah, my friend! At least I have you to talk to. My roommate isn't home, and even if she was, as I've mentioned to you a few times, I'm not that connected to her.

I feel a little childish writing to you right now. With so many real problems in the world, mine ends up being just loneliness. Selfish of me that it saddens me, but I can't help it.

Hope you are well. Sorry for any inconvenience.

Xoxo,

Black Rose"

I didn't send the email right away. My fingers hesitated. How pathetic I would seem! However, I didn't have a choice. If it wasn't him, it wouldn't be anyone else. And I already felt the pain of John's abandonment that day. And he, my Dark Angel, always, always made me feel better. I needed that piece of happiness. Finally, without much further thought, I hit the send button. Done. Now for the waiting again. How painful was the waiting!

But, relief! My wait didn't last long. Not even five minutes had passed when I received the notification of a new email. And even before I opened it, my heart had already let go of some of the weight it carried. And I no longer had to struggle to hold back the tears. I opened his message immediately.

"Black Rose,

Oh, my dear Rose, you never need to apologize for anything! On the contrary, I am extremely happy that you found in me someone you feel comfortable talking to.

I'm sorry that loneliness afflicts you right now and that it's so difficult for you to deal with it. If I could, I would hold you tight. In any case, feel my virtual hug. And know you've been heard.

The world's problems shouldn't make you feel bad for experiencing your own pain. I wish there was something I could do to help you. If there is, please let me know.

Why don't you take advantage of your anguish and turn it into art? Something tells me this will make you feel better.

Don't forget that even in this unconventional reality of our relationship, I care a lot about you.

Xoxo,

Dark Angel"

The crying from before, which was barely contained, suddenly turned into smiles. I felt calm, accepted. My dark angel never let me down. I didn't respond to his email right away. I didn't need to. Sleep was now beginning to envelop me. I hadn't even realized it was dark out. Slowly, I got up, put on my pajamas, and went to bed. I dove under the covers. I breathed. My eyes closed, and when they opened again, it was daylight. The sun streamed in through my window as if announcing a good omen.

⤜⤛ ⤜⤛

"So you want to know of all my experiences with the job market?" Alex asked in a curious tone. I felt a little uncomfortable with my own inquisitions, but I answered with a certain firmness.

"Only the things you think are most relevant. You know, as a trans woman, what peculiarities have happened to you in the corporate world?"

She laughed bitterly.

"Peculiarities..." she repeated. Then there was a pause that she seemed to fill with memories and thoughts. She continued. "To tell you the truth, I don't have that many experiences. In offices, I only have one. I went for an interview for a receptionist job. I had already transitioned, but I still hadn't changed my name on my documents and all. So when the HR lady called out a male name and I answered, she thought I didn't understand. I explained. She was visibly uncomfortable. The interview lasted less than five minutes. She said she would call me, but of course, she didn't."

I looked at my notebook, not sure of what to write. I scribbled random words: male name; transition; uncomfortable. I found the strength to stop staring at the notebook and turned to her again.

"There was the time I took my resume to the grocery store in my neighborhood. But much to my chagrin, the manager was a guy who went to school with me. Seeing me, he whispered something in the ear of one of the cashiers and they both laughed. I wanted to turn around and leave, but I was desperate for a job. I was young then, about seventeen, I think. So I went ahead. I said hi, no response. I explained that I saw the ad that they were hiring. I handed over the sheet of paper with my resume. He took a while to pick it up and used his fingertips only, as if it was a radioactive object. I thanked him and, when I was going to ask who knows what, in front of me, he threw it in the trash can nearby. The girl he'd whispered to put her hands over her mouth, barely holding back a laugh. I then ran out of there."

Whisper; laughter; trash can—I wrote down in my notebook. I looked at Alex but said nothing. You could see that she recognized my lament. I let her continue.

"I got my first jobs when I was still a 'boy,' so I had some experience. I worked as a teenager in a movie theater and as an assistant in a craft store. But when I started transitioning, it didn't matter—nor did the fact that I got top grades in school, nor the fact I knew computer stuff or spoke Spanish. I only managed to work again when I was passable."

"Sorry," I interrupted her, "passable?"

"Ah, yes, when I already looked completely feminine. You know, boobs, long hair, and all."

"I see."

"Even so, I only got informal part-time jobs, because I still hadn't managed to change my name. Only then did I get a real job."

I took more notes in my notebook.

"And how did you get the informal stuff?"

"Oh yeah... well, I became passable when I was about twenty-three. I met a guy who was a DJ and he got me a gig as a bartender. I stayed there for a long time, but somehow the owner of the bar discovered my 'secret identity' and found some excuse to fire me."

Bartender; gig; fired.

"Then I got to be a waitress, but it paid horribly. Basically, just tips. Then I was a bartender again at another place and, for a while, I worked as a barista at a coffee place."

"And what happened when you changed your name?"

Alex smiled with an expression I couldn't decipher. A little heartbreak mixed with resilience perhaps?

"I got a job as a waitress at a club, through the contacts I already had. I remember that the interview was very weird because the owner of the place only asked me normal things, like experience and availability and salary expectations... It was strange to me not to be asked what I had between my legs or what my 'real' name was or to be disgusted or laughed at."

We stopped for a moment, interrupted by a girl who asked us for directions. She wanted to know where the Psychology building was. Alex directed her, but I remained silent. I felt a little sick, even thinking for a moment that I might throw up. It must had been my blood pressure. A lump in my throat, a pang in my heart. A singular pain, pain that wasn't mine, but it hurt anyway. The girl left and Alex turned to me once more.

"Are you okay?" she asked in a worried tone.

I looked at her again, as if seeing her for the first time. She must have thought I was crazy because instead of answering her question, I kept staring at her face, counting her frown lines, wondering what stories her features had to tell.

"You are pale," she continued, snapping me out of my trance. "Do you need to go to the nurse?"

"Uh, no, no..." I replied. "I think my blood pressure might be a little low, that's all. It happens."

"Are you sure?"

"Oh, yes, I am. Thank you."

Alex didn't look too convinced. She took a bottle of water from her backpack and offered it to me. I took it. I chugged the water; only then did I realize that I was thirsty.

"If you want, we can continue later. Classes are about to start anyway," she said as I sipped the last drop of water from the bottle.

"We can do that. Would you mind meeting me over the weekend?" I asked, remembering that it was already Friday; another Friday.

"Yes, sure. I'll give you my number and we can arrange something."

I handed her my phone so she would add her number to my contacts, and as I did, I saw John arriving. He was back to wearing his leather jacket, as the colder days now allowed, and his hair, carefully cut before, was growing longer—the light-brown locks almost reaching his shoulders. He was so extremely handsome that, even after so many months, he still made me gasp.

"Hi, good morning," he greeted us as soon as he was close enough.

We answered his greeting—me with an enthusiastic smile and Alex with her eyes downcast, as usual.

"I'm working on our project," I explained to John after he sat down next to me and kissed me on the cheek. "Alex is being such a great help!"

He smiled soberly and, addressing her, said, "Thank you very much."

His tone wasn't very excited, but lately, he wasn't excited about much of anything, really, much less with anything college related. Alex only nodded in response.

"Anything good going on this weekend?" asked John. I was surprised. It'd been a while since we made plans together. He was always so busy with work that I was lucky to get to see him for a few hours on a Sunday afternoon.

"Well, Kat is having some friends over tomorrow. We're just gonna drink, listen to music, and hang out. If you want to stop by..."

"Sure, I'd love to!"

I felt like my heart jumped up and almost stopped in my throat. The feeling was so strong that it took a tremendous effort for me not to cry. Cry? Why? I'm not quite sure... but I held the urge back.

"And Alex, why don't you come too?" I managed to say after swallowing my tears.

She seemed to hesitate for a moment.

"Yeah, I guess, okay..." she said at last.

"Great! If you can, you can even come early and help me with the project a little more. If you don't mind, of course."

"Sure, it's no trouble at all."

"Perfect," said John, "I can't wait!"

We then went to our respective classes. I was still stunned. I would have my John the very next day! Obviously, I was deeply happy. But there was something else that shared room in my feelings. However, without knowing what, I ignored this "something else." I let myself feel only the sweet pleasure of fantasizing about the near future. I deserved to allow myself, with so much anguish and irresolution and disconsolation of not knowing what was going on in his head lately. I was, therefore, all delight. Just for a moment.

The loud music, a kind of Latin pop with a bit of hip hop, intoxicated me. Everyone was happy. Even Alex was dancing wildly, bumping into furniture now and then. Kat was kissing a guy on the couch. John was talking to some people about sports, I think. Everyone laughed. I was busy with my glass of beer and the laughter I could barely contain. I'd just swallowed some special mushrooms Kat's friends had brought to the party. They made everything so funny. Someone passed me a weed vape. I took a hit, coughed, breathed, drank more beer, laughed some more. Life was good.

"Clara, come dance!" It was Alex who was calling me. I went to her, and we let ourselves be taken by the pleasant rhythm of the music. Kat joined us too, and the three of us twirled around, moving our bodies as if in a sisterhood ritual. I found myself loving those women—all women. I loved myself too, and for a brief moment, I even forgot that John was there. For a momentary second, I didn't remember his existence. But the instant passed. I looked at his face, so beautiful. He was smiling and looking in my direction. I loved him too—now I knew. Should I tell him? Why not? But soon the thoughts strayed back to the rhythm of the melody that filled our surroundings.

We stayed there for a long time, Alex, Kat, and I. Songs started and ended and started again. We didn't get tired. I felt like my body could handle dancing all night. Some people joined us. John also came after a while. He was not a good dancer, but he didn't seem to mind. He moved next to me, bodies in dangerous proximity. He would run his hand through my hair every now and then, messing it up. I laughed at his silliness. At one point, he squeezed me tight, bringing me close to him. He kissed me, caressing my waist, pressing his body against mine. I could feel his enthusiasm. After the kiss, we continued dancing. He was getting looser and looser, one could see. He went dancing with other friends, making people laugh. He got close to Kat. They moved rhythmically to the music. I turned to Alex, we spun around hand in hand. As I turned from the twirl, my easy laugh suddenly broke.

It only took a few seconds, but I seemed to perceive the movements as if they were being made in slow-motion. John put his arms around my roommate and brought his face to hers, pulling her closer to him—as he had done to me just now. She looked confused; her face twitched a little. He came closer and, in an attempt to reach her lips, even brushed his nose against hers. Kat pushed him away. He tried to kiss her a second time. She pushed him away again, an expression of fury in her eyes.

After that, a mist of senses. I didn't quite understand what was happening around me—I felt Kat's sorry gaze and Alex's hands taking me by the arms and leading me to my room. I threw myself on the bed. The music was lower. I looked up at the white ceiling, but I didn't see much as tears were blinding my eyes. Alex lay down beside me; she hugged me. I heard the door open—it was Kat. She also lay there with me and hugged me too. We didn't say anything. Only my sobs were heard, interrupted by the upbeat music.

"He's gone." Kat broke the silence that remained after I calmed down a little. I just nodded.

He's gone. He's gone. Gone.

⤙⤙⤙ ⤚⤚⤚

It was the third time he called me, and it was still eleven in the morning. My head hurt like hell. My heart too. My eyes barely opened, full, aching—I could feel they were swollen without even having to look in the mirror. I didn't want to look in the mirror, face the sad, pathetic figure of my pain.

I had woken up around eight with the phone ringing. Alex was beside me and Kat had ended up sleeping on the floor. All of us were awakened by the sound of my phone. I showed the screen with his name to them and pressed "ignore." I put the device in silent mode, and we went back to sleep. I woke up and slept again dozens of times. About ten o'clock, I got up for good. The girls were still asleep.

I went to make some coffee. Some people had slept on the couch. Three missed calls on the cell phone. And a text.

"Clara, please call me back."

The images from the night before were vivid in my memory, but I didn't cry anymore. I think I'd used all my tears. I felt like breaking something. Or screaming. Instead, I contented myself with drinking my black coffee—bitter, to match the moment—and starting to clean the kitchen, which was a mess. And I cleaned. Obsessively, as if my life depended on it. At some point, it was all done. People were leaving to heal their hangovers. Alex stayed. And she and Kat showered me with encouraging words. That I was too good for him. That I would find someone else. That he was a son of a bitch. That I deserved better.

We sat there together, eating junk food and watching movies for the rest of the day. Alex left in the afternoon and said she would call me later. Kat had to work, but asked me to let her know if I needed anything. I was alone then. Eleven missed calls on my cell phone. Missed calls. Lost calls. Lost, like me.

I thought about emailing Dark Angel. He always made me feel better. It was nice to think that I still had that angel in my life now that I'd lost John—ah, the pain still unrelentingly burned! I opened the email app on my phone, and just as I was about to start writing, a knock on the door interrupted me.

I wasn't too surprised to see John. I thought maybe he'd show up. I stared at his beautiful face without saying anything. I didn't invite him in. I didn't feel like crying. Nor did I feel like slapping him in the face. Something had broken, and despite everything, it was sad. The ecstasy of before, with my heart racing to have him around, the easy smile, the sexual desire... dead. He too was silent, perhaps waiting for my reaction. When he realized that I would not break the silence, he began to speak.

"Clara, are you... are you okay?"

I had to think for a moment. Was I okay? No. But it wasn't all bad either. Which was a very strange feeling. I felt numb, cold, as if I was incapable of loving now. Before I could make any mention of responding, John continued.

"I wanted to apologize for yesterday. It wasn't nice of me to hit on your friend. I know we don't have anything serious, but still, I shouldn't have done this."

My expression must have changed, given my surprise. I went back inside, sat on the couch. He came after me, closing the door. He sat beside me. He took my hands:

"Are we good?" he asked.

"What?"

"You and I... can we keep going out? I love your company. I really like our hookups."

Rage. Pure rage. He could see it in my gaze as he let go of my hands and backed away a bit.

"We've been dating for months! We went on a trip together; I met your family...." My words left my lips in a stream, without much filtering. As if trying to understand the absurdity of our miscommunication.

"Well, yes, it's true, but..." he hesitated, looking for words. "We never talked about it. I thought we were having a casual relationship. I'm sorry you thought..."

"Do you see other people?" I interrupted him. I don't know the why of the question, but I couldn't help it. The words seemed to have a life of their own. They came out without thinking.

He didn't say anything. And with that, he said it all. I wanted to ask him a thousand questions, but there was no point. Not even if he could answer my questions.

"I thought you liked me..." I said more to myself. Nothing I said from then on would have any purpose.

"I do, Clara! I like you a lot! I just don't think we have a future together... I... I don't feel..."

My eyes darted to his face and then down to my crossed legs, then back to his face. I didn't want to, but I shed a single tear. Weak. Stupid. Rejected. Unlovable.

"No," I said after what felt like centuries of silence.

"No... what?" John asked with confused eyes. I enjoyed his uncertainty for a few long seconds.

"We're not good. And we're not going to keep going out."

He got up, eyes lowered.

"I understand. I'm sorry, Clara. You are an amazing woman who deserves to be happy."

"I know."

"*Dark Angel,*

I had my heart broken today. I'm sad, but also, which is extremely strange, relieved. Looking back, the relationship was not ideal. I thought we had a lot in common, but in fact, we had almost nothing in common. But still, it's been hard to feel so alone.

I shouldn't feel alone, because I have the support of friends, and I have you. But I still do. I can't help but think about the good parts of what I stupidly thought was a relationship. Silly, huh?

He just left my place. My life. And I'm empty. And tomorrow I'll see him at school. And I don't know how it's going to be, and this uncertainty consumes me. If by any chance he tries to approach me, I don't know if I'll have the strength to say no.

What pathetic words, which seem to come from the heart of a teenager. But no. An adult woman letting herself feel this way.

I don't know if I'm going to send you this email, actually. So personal. But I think I will because in these times you are one of the only lights in my life.

I hope your weekend was better than mine.

Xoxo,

Black Rose"

After sending the message, I felt a little better. Enough to let myself try to distract my head, at least. I watched videos of kittens on the internet. I smiled a little, who knew. I ignored Alex's call—I didn't want to think about anything right now. I sent her a text message explaining that we would talk tomorrow. Then, luckily, I managed to fall asleep.

I woke up in the middle of the night with a nightmare. After waking up, for a millisecond, I thought everything was fine. And then I remembered that John was no longer part of my life. A hit. I went to the bathroom and then to bed, having fallen asleep on the couch. Kat had covered me with a blanket, which I took with me to the bedroom. I quickly checked the time on my cell phone: three in the morning. On the dot. The witching hour, they say. Or the devil's hour? One day I would look it up. I set my alarm for six. I shut my eyes. I thought of John. Of Dark Angel. Of my friends. My family. My country—which one? I thought of myself. And then, of nothingness. And of everything. Of what was real and what was fantasy. How difficult it was to differentiate the two.

⇢⇢⇛ ⇚⇚⇠

"Y ou have a swollen face, but it's not that bad. Let's see, I have concealer in my bag."

Alex opened her makeup bag inside her backpack. She owned all kinds of makeup supplies, and always said she had a solution for everything in her vanity bag. She took the concealer out and applied it under my eyes, on the tip of my nose, and on a few other areas of my face. She was very focused as she spread the product with her fingers. It was the third time I had asked her how my face looked, if one could tell I had been crying for the past couple of days. She assured me that I had a "Monday face." Normal. As if I had spent the weekend partying and was now carrying the consequences of my inconsequences.

"There," she said at last when satisfied. She put away her things, leaving out only a small mirror, which she offered to me. I looked at my reflection. The skin was fine, no dark circles or anything. But the eyes were sad. Well, no one would look me in the eye anyway.

"Thanks," I said as I handed the mirror back to her. I then told her about the day before and how he perceived our relationship so differently from me. And that he had left without even trying anything. And that I missed him. She listened to me in silence, didn't say anything, not even when I finished talking. She just took my hands, squeezing my fingers, as if in a discreet hug. I returned her caress with gratitude.

"You know, there's nothing you can do now to ease the pain too much," she ended up saying, "only time heals these things. Cliché, huh? But it's very true. And your time will be even longer because he goes to school here."

I sighed. I was tired, and that was just the beginning of the journey. How to get over a guy I would see all the time? And in that place that, despite already calling home, I still didn't belong—and probably never would? Alex was right, though. I didn't have a choice. And how it hurts to wait for this much-needed time to pass! In that instant, I made sense of all the songs and poems and paintings about love. About loss. About pain.

"Yeah, I know," I replied only. Our hands were still joined, and they stayed that way until it was time to go to class. I said goodbye to her, and it was hard to let her fingers slip away from mine. But I went on. With slow steps, one at a time. Until I reached the classroom. Until I got to my desk. There was no sign of John, but he was always late. The teacher arrived. I looked around. The present faces oblivious to my yearnings—and I, to theirs. John hadn't arrived. He wouldn't for the rest of that day. Or the next many days. I suspected I wouldn't see him around for the rest of the school year.

"*Black Rose,*

I'm so sorry that you're sad and feeling lonely. I don't know you more than through words and art, but it's enough to know that whoever broke your heart made a terrible mistake.

I don't know if it consoles you, but I can't imagine anyone in this world who is worthy of your sensitivity and wonderfulness. And that's why it's normal for you to feel lonely. It's not fair, of course. But who can blame the lowly mortals for not being able to keep you company at such a high level?

When you see him at school, look at him with pity for having lost a soul as incredibly beautiful as yours. And for knowing that he will never be able to find anyone like you.

It is also normal for you to feel silly or 'pathetic.' After all, these mundane pains always make artists feel this way. Your depth is too much to handle. But you are, first and foremost, human. And with that comes all the adversities that our humanity carries. So don't be afraid to feel. And don't feel shame. You need this anguish. Use it. Make art. Bring it to your level of understanding.

Also, never forget that I'll be here. Any way you want. As often as you need. As intimately as you let me.

Oh, and if you ever get back into the arms of this poor bastard who left you, don't feel like you've failed. Sometimes we need certain caresses in the soul, in the ego, in the flesh... you have every right to give yourself some comfort. Just be sure to let go of it as soon as that need is satisfied. And let it be soon.

One more thing: write to me whenever you want or need to. Never hesitate to send me the emails that are your rants. I'm your friend, your dark angel. I'm here. Always.

Xoxo,

Dark Angel"

That was strange. I was expecting to feel that familiar comfort when reading his email. His words always satisfied me so much that it was even hard to breathe—a smother of happiness, a whiff of delight. But not this time. Suddenly, the fact that my dark angel was a faceless, nameless entity stood out like a slap in the face or an unexpected icy wave in a hitherto calm sea. Our relationship felt fake now. For a long time, I thought it was truer than all the others I had had in that country—even the one I had with John; but now I realized. So obvious.

I stood there looking at my cell phone screen for endless minutes. Although our relationship was illegitimate, it had never been dishonest. At least for my part, I reflected. I clicked on "reply."

"Dark Angel,

Thank you for your words. I think only time will make me feel better. Little by little. Thank you so much for letting me vent to you. And I appreciate you having such a positive image of me.

Usually, when I read an email from you, my heart instantly fills up with joy. This may even sound like an exaggeration, but your messages served as a remedy for pain. Or a drug for boring days.

However, this time, I have to confess that I didn't have that feeling. Do you still have it? (That is, if you ever felt that way)

I'm not sure why, but today I realized how platonic our relationship is. You are a tangle of pretty words and I am a tangle of scribbles and paintings that, for some reason, touch you.

Don't get me wrong, please. What you and I have is unique. You are unique. But you are Dark Angel. You have no name, no address, no face. And I am Black Rose. From the lost era of blogging. From the oblivion of the arts.

I don't know what to do with these new insights, really. But I just wanted to be honest with you. I

hope I don't hurt you with these new truths of mine.
It's the last thing I would want.

Xoxo,

Black Rose"

I sent the email and went to bed. What stood out in my sensations was serenity. I thought remorse or regret would overwhelm me after writing to him, but the truth is that I felt, for the first time in a long time, certain peace. None of the euphoria of yesteryear, when my heart felt like it wanted to explode, no. On the contrary: it was the tranquility of having no chains; I don't know. All I know is that I slept well that night. A heavy sleep. No dreams, no nightmares. Peaceful.

I got an A for my project on the inclusion of trans people in the job market in addition to being congratulated by the professor, who said he was impressed with my results. John had dropped out of the course, apparently, so I ended up doing everything myself. Not that he was much help, anyway. I felt almost accomplished and with the feeling that things were falling into place. How it had to be. That cliché...

Alex was waiting for me after class, and we went out to lunch to celebrate. And it was a meal filled with joy. Comfort too. We ordered food that brought good feelings. Food for the soul. I thanked her, once again, for helping me see—so I could pass on a little piece of her reality. She thanked me too. Then life goes on. Work. Home. Classes. Until the following weekend, rest of the proletarians.

It had been two weeks since Dark Angel had sent me anything. I thought he might have been offended by my last email. I don't know. I wasn't sad though. I let indifference, or whatever it was, take over. It was all right, in the end. This certainty was a crazy thing, and I didn't know where it came from. But it was all that mattered now. And also the real people, of flesh and blood, who were part of my life. People I touched, heard the sound of their laughter, smelled, and knew if they'd changed their perfume or their hairstyle. Alex and Kat and Elena and friends of friends, classmates, teachers, the janitor and the cleaning lady, the cashier at the grocery store, the bank clerk and my bosses, and my little one who depended so much on my care.

So I let the days go by without hoping or longing too much. Without obsessing over the clock ticking. Without visiting the future so many times, and for so long. Learning to breathe. It wouldn't last forever, of course, the lull. But it's okay. Everything dies. And everything is born. And dies again. The resurrection was as real as the spins of the earth.

>>>>> <<<<<

I finally received the email. I didn't open it right away, wondering if it would be the last. The ending is always a little sad, after all. But I plucked up my courage in the end.

"Black Rose,
I really appreciate your sincerity. I think our relationship doesn't deserve less than that, right? And I never doubted your honesty in writing to me, of course, but this email was further proof of the transparency that exists here.
I confess that I deliberately delayed giving you an answer. Mostly because I didn't quite know what to say. I was sad. I thought I wouldn't even write you anything else, just let it go. But how to let it go? I don't know.
You asked me if I felt that joy or euphoria that you described in your message. Yes. I still do. There are few feelings so intense in everyday life and your words and especially your art fill me with the ecstasy that I believe we all seek in life.

But the feeling slipped away from you. And I understand your whys. For a while, it's a lot easier to trust someone who wears a mask and an alias, of course. But then the 'real' reality ends up facing us. More is needed. A fact. An identity. A face.

So, my dear Black Rose, I offer you more, if that's what you need now. My name is Thomas Jones. I am forty-one years old. I live in New York City. I'm divorced. I've attached a photo of myself and I'll leave the links to my profiles on social media. You can know what you want from me. If it's not on the internet, feel free to ask me here.

I won't wait for an answer from you, but if I get one anyway, I'll be very happy. Take care. Always.

Xoxo,
Dark Angel"

I was a little shocked. I didn't expect Dark Angel—Thomas—to reveal his identity. I opened the photo. He was completely different from what I had imagined. Well, actually, I'd never tried to form a picture of him in my head, but if I had, it wouldn't be the one that the open image on my cell phone screen reflected. He had black hair and a clean beard; striking features; his eyes were small but intense, and his lips were well contoured and full.

He was very handsome. A charm like you see in Hollywood actors—like Antonio Banderas, I think.

I didn't want to reveal him even more, but my curiosity won. I looked at his social media. Pictures of trips, political opinions, art, photos of pets, recommendations for songs to work out to. Perfection. Lots of friends. Thomas Jones. No more Dark Angel.

I closed the open apps, dropped the phone on the couch. Thomas. Thomas... I suddenly didn't know who he was anymore. Now I had all the information I could ever want, but the certainties from before, of my dark angel, were gone. Dark Angel had words, sensitivity. Thomas had friends, dogs, a job. They were two different people in my head. And I didn't know this new individual, Thomas Jones. I wasn't even sure if I wanted to.

I left my phone right there and ran to my room. I opened my drawers. Paper, pencil. I scribbled it down, without thinking, as it always was. Flow of feelings that, even though they came from me, were more observed than felt. Scribble, scribble... Thomas. Dark Angel. The fluidity of pencil over paper. The flood of unconsciousness. Then I stopped. And the pencil was now resting on the table. The drawing was of an angel. A dark angel, of course. He flew away, colossal wings spread in motion. His face could not be seen. He was naked. His back was turned. Slipping away...

I then returned to the living room. I took my cell phone, that tool of experiences. I replied to him, a bit of grief laced in me.

"Dark Angel,
Dark Angel. Can I still call you that?
I do not know what to say. I didn't expect you to open up to me like that. For me. Please give me time to absorb so much information. I will write to you soon.
Xoxo,
Black Rose"

Time passed—populated with the most anecdotal moments.

First came Halloween. Kat took me to her hometown in New Jersey for a weekend, and we went apple and pumpkin picking on a real farm; nothing more picturesque for the big-city girl I was. A wagon took us to the plantations. There were many children and families around us. Good Vibes. It was cold, but a cozy little sun made it bearable. We bought two bags at the market that belonged to the farm and filled them with apples, as many as we wanted. Kat ate some right there. Then we went to pick pumpkins—one each. The field had them as far as the eye could see.

After that, we had apple cider—warm, unlike any drink I'd ever tasted—and donuts, also made out of apples. Kat explained to me that it was a typical thing at the time. They had everything in that flavor: ice cream, cakes, pies... Sitting at the outdoor tables next to the market, we saw children enjoying their treats, and some were happily running after playing at the offered activities: a cornfield maze, a place with animals that they could interact with, a giant bounce house. I kept thinking about how little Clara would have fun in that place. I often thought about the childhood things I would have had if I had grown up in that country—but also about the things I would have missed.

We went back to Kat's parents' house. They were extremely sweet and hospitable, bordering on uncomfortable at times. I didn't know how to react to such displays. Her mother used the apples to make a pie, which we later ate with vanilla ice cream. The pumpkins were destined to become jack-o'-lanterns. We took the "innards" of the pumpkin out by cutting the top of the vegetable. My fingers and clothes and surroundings were covered in the orange "guts." I almost felt like a surgeon. Then, with sharp-edged knives, we cut the "face" of our creation. I followed the classic design of pumpkins that we see in the movies. Kat decided to make hers with a scarier face, a wide mouth full of teeth, and demonic eyes. We put LED candles inside our pumpkins and arranged our creations by the front door of the house. At night, we could see the glowing eyes that creepily lit up the surroundings. I asked myself if I had ever felt, in that country, so immersed in the culture. And that night I went to sleep with a good feeling—of belonging.

It had been almost a month since my last email to Dark Angel—or rather, Thomas. It was weird not talking to him for so long, especially knowing it had been my choice. However, there was the balsam of freedom that I felt so strongly now. Freedom from what? From the dependence on the sensations he brought me, perhaps. But there was also an emptiness, and these feelings all mixed up together during my days and nights.

>>>>> <<<<<

One day, it was Thanksgiving. The end of November was already pushing away the dry leaves and bringing the cold that heralded the imminent arrival of winter. I wasn't looking forward to the change of seasons. There were even some signs of snow on certain days.

That holiday, at Kat's insistence, we went back to New Jersey to spend with her family. Not just her parents this time. The celebration was to bring families together, just like Christmas. I met her uncles and aunts and cousins. I met her younger sister, married and obscenely pregnant. And also a few outsiders, friends of the family—my category, I suppose. We were at her uncles' house, the host that year. He had a husband and two tiny, furry puppies: a cliché. Everyone was all dressed up. Every person brought something to contribute to dinner. I bought some wine and made dessert: *pavê*; they found it quite exotic and called the dish a "trifle."

The entire time people were interacting before dinner, the television was on for a football game. Kat told me it was part of the tradition, not just for her, but for the rest of the country. Apparently, it was an important game. I believe that only the children shared my indifference to the score. So I spent a lot of time playing with them. It was so much easier to connect. Adults, ah, make you walk on eggshells, weighing your words and manners. And they had their curiosities, but it was impolite to ask questions. As for the children, without filters, they didn't hesitate to question my funny accent, or why I wasn't watching the game, and what was my favorite song, and where was this Brazil place I said I was from. The parents, from time to time, told them to stop bothering me, but I'd make a gesture, assuring them everything was fine and, one could tell, they thanked heavens, and went back to their wines and their game.

Dinner was served around five in the afternoon. I was surprised we'd eat so early but didn't question it. We all sat at the table, except the children, who had a smaller table just for them. I wasn't very hungry as I had been eating appetizers most of the day: cheese and crackers, chips, vegetables, and fruit. Even so, I put a little of everything on my plate to try. I had never seen some of those foods: cranberry sauce; mashed potatoes with marshmallows; yams; mac and cheese; something called stuffing, that I'm not sure what it was made of; and, of course, the main dish, the turkey. One of Kat's uncles, the owner of the house, carved it as if it were part of a religious ceremony: standing, solemn, slowly. Everyone toasted after the first cut.

The mix of sweet and salty foods was a little strange, but I really liked the flavors. For dessert, everyone wanted to try my *pavê* and praised my culinary skills. I had a piece of pumpkin pie with whipped cream. And then we went back to the living room to drink some more. Someone suggested that we play the game of saying what we were thankful for that day. After all, the meaning of the holiday was this: to give thanks. Everyone's gratitude was more of the same: thank you for my family, for the food on the table, for my health... The children were grateful that Christmas was coming and for their parents and their toys. When it was my turn, I said what was expected. I'm grateful for my family and friends and blah blah blah... but I thought to myself: what I was really grateful for were art and emancipation.

I t was cold that morning. I had to pull my winter coat out of the back of my closet, which I had bought as soon as I arrived in the country, almost a year ago. I should get into the building, which had heat, but I wanted to spend some time in the sun. There were few people walking around the campus at that hour, but you could see some carrying their hot coffee or running in their gym clothes and coats, an excitement beyond my mundane comprehension.

I also had my coffee cup, which now rested beside me on the concrete bench. I took occasional sips while reading a book. It was a romantic novel with epic encounters and moments of surprise that accompanied the heroine's life, who was beautiful, chaste, kind, of course. And the hero, her crush, brave, noble, and generous. Easy words, simple narrative; a book that someone like Alex would never waste time reading. But I was tired of reflections and depths and very intense feelings. I wanted to be entertained while kissed by the sun and embraced by the frigid morning air.

"Hi, Clara."

The familiar voice interrupted my reading. I didn't react right away. I kept thinking that maybe it was my imagination. But no. There was John, standing in front of me, same leather jacket, same haircut. The only difference in his figure was the slightly overgrown beard. His scent was also the same; how had I not noticed it before?

I set the book aside, next to my coffee, slowly. I remembered, for a fraction of a second, when he was the one who brought me coffee before classes. Not this time. Not in a long time. I made my coffee at home. Brazilian coffee. And I bought a reusable cup. The taste was much better than the ones he used to bring me long ago.

"Hi," I replied, no doubt showing questions in my eyes. I waited for him to say something in return, but he just smiled. A rather weak, awkward smile. And so I went on. "What are you doing here?"

"I'm thinking about resuming the course next year, and I came to talk to them, see what I have to do."

"Oh..."

We stood there, the two of us, like two lost kids, not talking for longer than we could bear. His hands opened and closed, seeming to wield an invisible I-don't-know-what every millisecond. My heart was pounding, but not the way it used to. I no longer felt the lust, the fantasy, the attraction that I used to have. But what John had been, what I had been, still shook me, no doubt.

"Do you want to have some coffee?" he said, a little hesitantly.

"I already have mine," I replied promptly, pointing to my cup and even taking a sip before putting it back on the bench. I continued, "Besides, I don't think this would be a good idea."

"You're right. Good to see you, Clara. Take care."

"You, too."

I watched John turn around, a little embarrassed—or perhaps it was just my imagination—and I saw his silhouette getting smaller and smaller until he disappeared in the distance. I grabbed my book, my backpack, and my coffee and went inside; I was tired, now, of the cold.

><≪

I t's funny how certain things happen all at once. The same day I was surprised by John's presence, I received an email from Dark Angel. I didn't open his message right away, but that night, alone in my room, a glass of wine in hand, I decided to face his words.

"Black Rose,
I know I should wait for your answer, but the truth is, I can't contain myself any longer. I've held back too much not to send you this email earlier and I feel like the anxiety is going to kill me.

I don't know if I'm in a position to ask you anything, but I think our relationship gives me some opening to do so. I could be wrong, I don't know. But I'll try anyway.

I know you need something more than the platonic nature of our relationship. I think I do too, to some extent. And I thought that by giving you my name, face and all, that would be settled. But it was naive on my part. Even with the information you have now about me, I'm just an online persona. Some photos, some posts on social media, I don't know.

It seems obvious now, I know, but the obviousness has been eluding me lately. I think the more emotions there are, the harder it is to think rationally, you know? And you have art, but I have nothing. Therefore, forgive me for failing to recognize the gap that exists between your needs and what I have offered you. So, my dear Black Rose, what I want to give you is my presence. I don't know where you are. But if not so close, we can meet halfway. Or I can come to you. Whatever works for you. That's the only possible ending to our story, don't you think?

I am waiting for your reply.

Xoxo,

Thomas"

Thomas. Not Dark Angel anymore. I stared at his name at the end of the email, obsessing over it. A sip of red wine. Thomas. Thomas... thomas. I turned off the cell phone screen, went back to reading my book. But the name still echoed inside my mind. An uncomfortable reverberation. An annoying repetition. A void.

A little bit more
of winter

T he first snowstorm of the season arrived two days before Christmas. The city was covered with the mantle of whiteness. The landscape was beautiful when seen from the windows, away from the pollution of the streets. The dry branches of the trees were covered too, like the Christmas pines in Brazil that use cotton to imitate snow. During the day, you could see little children having snowball fights, which exploded into a thousand particles when they hit their target. Or they built snowmen; most of them quite small and ugly, but every now and then you would find a big beautiful one like in the movies.

That morning we decided to make hot chocolate. Alex had bought mini marshmallows when she went to the store the day before, just for that purpose. Kat melted the chocolate in warm milk, then poured the drink into three glasses. She completed her art with whipped cream and marshmallows on top. We had it with chocolate chip cookies, which I had made the day before. A breakfast as sweet as the taste of good news.

The three of us sat on the floor of the living room, which was covered with a fluffy carpet. Alex insisted we get a carpeted apartment. We were lucky to find this one, which a friend of Kat's was renting us. Three quite large bedrooms, a kitchen with a dishwasher and two bathrooms. We turned on the TV and watched a cooking show; it was kind of a tradition when the three of us were off and we woke up early enough.

"We could make ham for Christmas dinner," Alex suggested after taking a sip of her chocolate.

"Or turkey," I said.

Christmas Eve would be the very next day, and we still hadn't decided what to do for food. If it was up to Kat, we'd order pizza or Chinese food, but Alex made a point of cooking dinner, with the table set and all. And I... I was happy just to have their company.

C hristmas Eve was a very different thing from what I was used to. In Brazil, we stayed up until after midnight—my family, in particular, insisted on eating only then. There was music. Everyone dressed up, wore new clothes, even if it was to stay home. We ate turkey, pork, chicken salad, endless desserts. And we opened the gifts.

My evening with the girls was a four o'clock dinner, wearing those tacky Christmas sweaters and drinking. The gifts were all under the Christmas tree and wouldn't be opened until the next morning. They told me that kids get up very early on Christmas Day and there are chocolate chip and cinnamon pancakes and families like to wear matching pajamas.

After eating, we watched Christmas-themed movies—another American tradition, I learned. Alex was asleep in five minutes. Kat and I finished the second movie and decided it was time for bed.

That night, I dreamed, like when I was a child, about the arrival of this Santa Claus guy. Ah, the symbol of rampant capitalism, but which managed to make the end of the year so sweet. He was not an old man dressed in red in the dawn of my unconsciousness, however. He wore, instead, a white coat, which blended in with the snow on the ground and made him look like he was floating, even. His back was turned, and I called out his name—I don't know what name, I don't remember, but it wasn't one by which this mythical being was usually known. He turned and smiled at me, and I realized he was actually a woman. Young in face, but with white hair and a protruding belly. I smiled back and she went on her way. I woke up with a sense of peace.

As soon as I opened my eyes, I noticed that there was some movement around the house. The girls had already woken up. A good smell came from the kitchen—coffee and cinnamon. I got up, put on my slippers, and went to them, who were in the living room, eating their pancakes and drinking their cups of coffee while watching the news on TV.

"Good morning," Alex said, smiling, as she saw me. "Merry Christmas!"

"Merry Christmas," I replied, addressing the two of them.

"There are pancakes and coffee in the kitchen," Kat said. "We've been waiting for you to open presents."

I went to get my breakfast. Black Brazilian coffee. Cinnamon pancakes with maple syrup and butter. I sat with them on the living room floor, and we ate together. I was happy. On television, reports on the Christmas spirit—lots of people feeding the hungry, giving gifts to the little children without parents, giving and giving... I wish Christian humanity was like this all year round. But I internally refused to complain. The gratitude of being there to see such acts of kindness melted my heart a little and chased away my cynicism.

After eating, we sat by the tree. Kat was distributing gifts according to the names we put on the packages. There were many. I discovered early on that Americans love to cram their Christmas trees. They told me that in homes where there are children, it is even more absurd. I told them that in Brazil we only got one gift from each person—if that. At least, that's how I grew up in my lower-middle-class home.

I got painting supplies: brushes, canvases, paints, an art history book. Also earrings, a scarf, pajamas, shirts. For Alex, I gave an English translation of *Dom Casmurro* by Machado de Assis, an eyeshadow palette, cute little trinkets I found in department stores. For Kat, clothes, a bottle of her favorite wine, and a purse.

After exchanging gifts, they got ready to leave. They would spend the rest of the day with their respective families. They both invited me to accompany them, but I decided I preferred to be alone. I made a video call with my family in Brazil, then had leftovers from last night's dinner for lunch. I took a long bath, listened to music, read. It no longer bothered me to be alone. Late in the afternoon, a light blizzard began to fall. I could almost see the snowflakes in their infinite individuality. It was beautiful. The sun was already setting, always early in the winter, and the landscape had orange colors that mixed with the white of the ice crystals, almost transparent so soft was their appearance.

I opened one of my new canvases. No rush, no ambitions. I got my paints and my brushes. My fingers slid them across the canvas smoothly, freely. And I portrayed that peculiar sky in my art. It wasn't *mine*, in fact, it was nature's. But that was okay. In the end, even what came from my imagination to canvases or pieces of paper was of the world first. I was just an instrument.

I spent New Year's Eve at a bar. I think it was my most fun experience of all that time in the States. The girls and I dressed up together, listening to music, creating elaborate makeup looks, with lots of glitter and lots of color. Unlike in Brazil, it was not traditional to wear white, but I did it anyway. I explained to them some of the things we did for luck for the following year: eating lentils, jumping seven waves on the beach... They were very intrigued. There wasn't much of it here; it was just another celebration. There were, of course, the end-of-year resolutions. Kat said she wanted to lose I-don't-know-how-many pounds. Alex said she would read more, not just the required college books. And I, unlike in previous years, did not think of any resolution. For the first time, I tried to enter a new phase without much expectation. Living one day at a time. We'd see how that works...

The bar was very crowded. It wasn't quite a club, but there was a small dance floor and a stage, which, that night, would be filled with drag queen lip-sync shows. The bar was LGBTQIA+, and Alex used to work there as a bartender a few years back. The music varied between what was playing on the radio at the time and classic pop songs. A lot of people were already dancing, clearly having started the celebrations very early. We ordered some special drinks that Alex knew about. She introduced us to everyone who worked behind the bar. Even with the loud music, we managed to talk a little. How many lives, how many stories and colors and pains and private worlds. I was moved. And happy. And already a little drunk.

When the shows started, the whole crowd went to the front of the stage. Passionate beings danced to Cher and Madonna and Whitney. I was included. The colored lights matched the extravagance of the rest of the whole. I danced until my legs hurt and laughed until my stomach hurt. Some of the artists performed more comical and caricatured shows, while others were more serious. After a few performances, there was a break, and the songs were played by the DJ again. And we went to sit for a while at a table. I grabbed a beer, thinking I should take a break from the cocktails. And I was thirsty too.

Kat couldn't stop thanking Alex for suggesting that bar. I was also filled with gratitude. How difficult it was, sometimes, to leave the "important" things in life in the background and just feel the simple pleasures of a good laugh, for example. There was no price for the privilege of being able to forget one's anxieties, even if only for a night, a moment, among so many moments that exist in each one's existence.

Midnight did not take long to arrive. We did the countdown along with the TV, turned on to the broadcast of Times Square. I had even considered spending New Year's there, but the intense cold discouraged me. Besides, that year, it was raining—which didn't stop the place from being as crowded as ever. As we counted backwards and the ball dropped, I kept thinking about how crazy that year had been; I wondered if everyone else was thinking about it; if not about the past, probably about the future. We always hope that the time that is coming will be better than the one already gone. But who knows? We can only wait.

At midnight, a shower of confetti, hugs, and kisses. The champagne glasses were touching, some gently, others so strongly that the liquid spilled onto anyone nearby—not that anyone cared. In addition to the melody of the glasses, you could also hear horns and screams and lots of "Happy New Year." I drank my champagne, which was actually prosecco, and hugged my friends, one on each side. Kat went looking for someone to kiss on the mouth, a country tradition. Alex went dancing when the music came on again. And I sat there at the bar, watching the euphoria of the hopeful beings that were there. Hopeful for a better year.

The month of January flew by—as fast, as high in the sky as the eagle Americans use as their symbol. And, like the majestic and frightening bird, no one seemed to notice that time was passing under our noses. In Brazil, my friends were getting ready for the upcoming Carnaval. And I held back the nostalgia for the street parties of São Paulo and had to be content with watching the samba school parades on television. Or, more likely, on the computer.

In the United States, people looked forward to Valentine's Day. Stores were decked out with red and pink hearts, and TV commercials showed you what gifts to buy your significant other that would make them fall in love with you even more. The children also participated in it, making little cards and exchanging small gifts with their schoolmates. Here, not only couples were presented, but also friends, relatives, teachers, and so on. It was kind of a love day. I liked the concept, although in practice I knew that the biggest consumers of the date were those who were in a romantic relationship.

Impossible, then, not to think about the inevitable loneliness of being single. Every now and then, it came to me. I wasn't unhappy about it, but sometimes, on a dark night or a nice day, I thought it would be good to have a boyfriend to keep me company. Inevitable, too, to think about my recent past and wonder what John was doing. I had blocked him from social media, and he never posted anything anyway. I wondered if he was with anyone. I felt a little sorry for that person. But maybe he'd be good for her. Maybe with someone else, he'd be different.

I also thought, of course, about Dark Angel, as these two men were kind of intertwined in my life. How crazy that had all been. The observer in me had known it all along, of course, but now the truth was so clear I don't know how my past self didn't see it.

I was at work. As the baby took her afternoon nap, I was overcome with nostalgia or I-don't-know-what, and I opened the email app on my phone. I typed in the search "Dark Angel." A few seconds of searching, loading, loading... it was taking so long, I thought, on top of my modern habits. Done. The results. One email. The last one. It was a little sad, but also very liberating. I opened it.

"Dark Angel,
It was a pleasure to share part of my journey with you. May your flight take you to places never imagined—not even by the fanciful minds of artists.
Xoxo,
Black Rose"

I'd reread my reply to his last email over and over again—when the nostalgia hit—sometimes to remind myself, sometimes to reassure myself (of what?), sometimes for no specific reason. Just to not let what had been die once and for all—or, perhaps, to mourn what inevitably died? I don't know. But it felt good, somehow. Looking at the past every now and then made me get back to the present.

So many holidays have come and gone. So many seasons. Art. Dates. College exams. The dance that life does when the Earth spins. I understood a little more, but still, I knew nothing. The mess in my room said so—handouts thrown on the table ("The North American Job Market," "The Psychology of Human Resources") shared space with sketches of drawings on scraps of paper. Some of my paintings were hanging on the wall, and others were tucked away in the back of my closet—along with my suitcases. My bookshelf was crammed with books, even poetry, and also with dirty makeup brushes—there were also the picture frames, though you could barely see them: a picture of me alone, one with the little girl I cared for, one of my family (mother, father, brother) and one with Alex and Kat, which we had taken on a beautiful sunny day in Central Park.

The distant graduation was now not so far away. And I had reflections and decisions to make. But not yet. For now, I looked out my bedroom window, into the dark night. The city lights illuminated its hurrying people—few, but still there—and their noisy vehicles. But inside, a smell of meatloaf, a sound of laughter muffled by the thick walls. A call.

"Clara, Alex finished dinner, come eat!"

I closed the blinds on my window and smiled, breathing in the aroma of homemade food, already anticipating the taste of the meal. Of communion. My footsteps guided me to the already set table. Kat poured me some wine, and before we ate, the three of us toasted.

"To friendship," Alex proposed.

"To friendship," we replied as our glasses clinked.

As we ate, we chatted about the relevant banalities of life. Kat would have a date with someone she met on an app. Alex told us about the job interview she'd had earlier. Who had seen the new show on that streaming service? Tomorrow the day will be beautiful. Did you know that so-and-so, that actor, died? The presidential elections were chaotic. We could have a picnic this weekend; it would be warm...

Inside, the blackness of the night did not come. Protected from the serene cold, from bad intentions, from distances and proximities, I felt good. I didn't know what it would be, of course, but the solace of being was enough for me—for now.

About the Author

Born and raised in São Paulo, Brazil, Dani Santos Lang made her first attempts to express herself through writing at the age of eight. Since then, between prose and poetry, she has not stopped writing.

She published her first poem, *"Noite Fria"*, in 2007, through a contest, in the collection *"Panorama da Literatura Brasileira Contemporânea – Poemas selecionados – Volume I"*. Also in 2007, she had two chronicles read on a local radio station.

In 2010, she published the poem *"Entre a rima e o discurso"* in the online version of the *Continuum Itaú Cultural* magazine, November-December edition.

She graduated in Language and Literature in 2011 and, in 2013, moved to the United States, where she wrote her first book, "Girls who talk or stories from all of us", with the first edition (in Portuguese) published in 2020.

In the US, she began to venture into writing in English as well. Her second book, "Affections in the Star-Flagged Land", was the first to get its English version. Navigating between two languages and two experiences, Dani continues her endless journey through the world of literature.